"I'm very glad you came back safely."

Blake Chandler smiled bitterly in response to his wife's cool welcome. "Really, Dina?" he mocked. "Then why do I get the feeling that you wish I'd died in the jungle?"

"I don't!" Dina protested. "I want to love you again, Blake," she admitted huskily. "But we both need time to adjust."

She knew it would be harder for her than for Blake. Blake would once again take over as president of the Chandler hotel chain. She would have to give up her identity as Dina Chandler, businesswoman, for that of Mrs. Blake Chandler, wife. The wife of a man she no longer even knew!

JANET DAILEY AMERICANA

STRANGE
BEDFELLOW

Harlequin Books

TORONTO • NEW YORK • LONDON
AMSTERDAM • PARIS • SYDNEY • HAMBURG
STOCKHOLM • ATHENS • TOKYO • MILAN

The state flower depicted on the cover of this book is
violet.

Janet Dailey Americana edition published January 1988
Second printing October 1988

ISBN 373-21939-3

Harlequin Presents edition published July 1979
Second printing February 1982

Original hardcover edition published in 1979
by Mills & Boon Limited

CHAPTER ONE

THE AIR WAS CLEAR and the moon over Rhode Island was new, but there was a tangle of cobwebs in her mind. Dina Chandler couldn't seem to think her way out of the confusion. She shut her ears to the voices quietly celebrating in other parts of the house and stared out the window.

A shudder passed through her. It couldn't have been from the night's chill, since the house was comfortably heated. Her blue eyes slid to her arms, crossed in front of her, hugging her middle. Perhaps it was the cold weight of the precious metal around her finger.

Dina turned from the window. Her restless gaze swept the library, noting all that was familiar. Interrupting the dark, richly paneled sides of the room was a wall of bookshelves, floor to ceiling. A myriad of deeply toned bindings formed rows of muted rainbows. A sofa covered in antique velvet faced the fireplace, flanked by two chairs upholstered in a complementing patterned fabric. In a corner of the room stood a mahogany desk, its top neat and orderly.

The door to the library opened and Dina turned. Her hair shimmered in the dim light, a paler gold than the ring on her finger. A pang of regret raced through her that her solitude had been broken, fol-

lowed by a twinge of remorse that she had felt the
need to be alone at this time.

Closing the door, Chet Stanton walked toward
her, smiling despite the faintly puzzled gleam in his
eyes.

"So this is where you've got to," he murmured,
an unspoken question behind the indulgent tone.

"Yes," Dina nodded, unaware of the sigh in her
voice, or how forced her smile looked.

As he came closer, her gaze made a detached
inspection of him. Like hers, his coloring was fair,
sandy blond hair falling rakishly across his forehead, always seeming to invite fingers to push it
back in place. His eyes were a smoke blue as
opposed to the brilliant shade of hers.

At thirty-six, he was twelve years her senior, a
contemporary of Blake's, but there was a boyish air
about him that was an integral part of his charm. In
fact, it was with Blake that Dina had first met Chet.
The cobwebs spun around that thought to block it
out. Slim and supple, Chet was only a few inches
taller than she was in her heels.

He stopped in front of her, his intent gaze study-
ing her expressionless face. Dina was unconscious
of how totally she masked her inner turmoil. As his
hands settled lightly on her shoulders, she was passive under his touch.

"What are you doing in here?" Chet cocked his
head slightly to the side, his gaze still probing.

"I was thinking."

"That's forbidden." His hands slid around her
and Dina yielded to his undemanding embrace,
uncrossing her arms to spread them across his
chest.

Why not? His shoulder had become a familiar resting place for her head, used often in the last two and a half years. Her eyes closed at the feathery caress of his lips over her temple and cheek.

"You should be in the living room noisily celebrating with the others," he told her in mock reproof.

Dina laughed softly in her throat. "They're not 'noisily' celebrating. They don't 'noisily' do anything, whether it's rejoice or grieve."

"Perhaps not," he conceded. "But even a restrained celebration should have the engaged couple in attendance, namely you and me. Not just me alone."

"I know," she sighed.

His shoulder wasn't as comfortable as it had seemed. Dina turned out of his unresisting embrace, nerves stretching taut again as the niggling sense of unease and confusion wouldn't leave. Her troubled gaze searched the night's darkness beyond the windowpanes as if expecting to find the answer there.

With her back turned to him, she felt Chet resting his hands on either side of her neck, where the contracted cords were hard bands of tension.

"Relax, honey. You've let yourself get all strung up again." His supple fingers began working their magic, gently kneading the coiled muscles in her neck and shoulders.

"I can't help it." A frown puckered her forehead despite the pleasant manipulations of his hands. "I simply don't know if I'm doing the right thing."

"Of course you are."

"Am I?" A corner of her mouth lifted in a half

smile, self-mocking and skeptical. "I don't know how I let you talk me into this engagement."

"Me? Talk *you* into it?" Chet laughed, his warm breath fanning the silver blond strands of her hair. "You make it sound as if I twisted your arm, and I'd never do that. You're much too beautiful to risk damaging."

"Flatterer!" But Dina felt old, old beyond her years.

"It got me you."

"And I know I agreed willingly to this engagement," she admitted.

"Willingly but hesitantly," added Chet, continuing the slow and relaxing massage of her shoulders and neck.

"I wasn't sure. And I still don't know if I'm sure."

"I didn't rush you into a decision. I gave you all the time you wanted because I understand why you felt you needed it," he reasoned. "And there won't be any marriage until you set the date. Our agreement is a little more than a trial engagement."

"I know." Her voice was flat. Dina didn't find the necessary reassurance in his words.

"Look—" Chet turned her to face him "—I was Blake's best friend."

Yes, Dina thought. He had been Blake's right arm; now he was hers. Always there, ready to support her decision, coaxing a smile when her spirits were low and the will to go on had faded.

"So I know what kind of man your husband was," he continued. "I'm not trying to take his place. As a matter of fact, I don't want to take his place any more than I want you to take his ring from your finger."

His remark drew her gaze to the intertwining gold band and diamond solitaire on the third finger of her left hand. The interlocking rings had been joined by a third, a diamond floret designed to complement the first pair. It was Chet's engagement ring to her.

He curved a finger under her chin to lift it. "All that I'm hoping is that with a little more patience and persistence I can carve some room in your heart to care for me."

"I do, Chet," Dina stated. "Without you, I don't know how I would have made it through those months when Blake was missing—when we didn't know if he was alive or dead. And when we were notified that he'd been kil—"

The rest of her words were silenced by his firm kiss. Then he gathered her into his arms to hold her close, molding her slenderly curved shape to his lean, muscular body.

His mouth was near her temple, moving against her silken hair as he spoke. "That's in the past. You have to forget it."

"I can't." There was a negative movement of her head against his. "I keep remembering the way I argued with Blake before he left on that South American trip," she sighed. "He wanted me to go to the airport with him, but I refused." Another sigh came from her lips, tinged with anger and regret. "Our quarrels were always over such petty things, things that seem so stupid now."

"The strong vying with the strong." Chet lifted his head to gaze at the rueful light in her eyes. "I'm partial to strong-minded women."

His teasing words provoked the smile he sought. "I suppose I have to admit to being that, don't I?"

A fire smoldered in his look, burning away the teasing light. "And I love you for being strong, Dina." His hand slid to the small of her back. "And I love you for being all woman."

Then his mouth was seeking hers again in a kiss that was warm and passionate. She submitted to his ardor, gradually responding in kind, reveling in the gentle caress of his hands that remained short of intimate. Chet never demanded more from her than she was willing to give. His understanding restraint endeared him to her, making her heart swell with quiet happiness.

When he lifted his head, Dina nestled into the crook of his arm, resting her cheek against his shoulder, smiling with tender pleasure. That lock of hair, the color of sun-bleached sand, was across his forehead. She gave in to the impulse to brush it back with the rest, knowing it would spring forward the instant it was done. Which it did.

"Feel better?" His fingers returned the caress by tracing the curve of her cheekbone.

"Mmm."

"What were you thinking about when I came in?"

Her hand slid to his shirt, smoothing the collar.

"I don't know. I guess I was wishing."

"Wishing what?"

Dina paused. She didn't know what she had been wishing. Finally she said, "That we hadn't told the others about our engagement, that we'd kept it to ourselves for a while. I wish we weren't having this engagement party."

"It's just family and friends. There's been no official announcement made," Chet reminded her.

"I know." She usually had no difficulty in expressing herself, but the uncertainty of her own thoughts made it impossible.

Something was bothering her, but she didn't know what it was. It wasn't as if she hadn't waited a proper time before deciding to marry again. It had been two and a half years since Blake had disappeared and a little more than a year since the South American authorities had notified her that they had found the plane wreckage and there had been no survivors.

And it wasn't as if she didn't love Chet, although not in the same tumultuous way she had loved Blake. This was a quieter and gentler emotion, and probably deeper.

"Darling—" his smile was infinitely patient "—we couldn't keep our engagement from our family and friends. They need time, too, to get adjusted to the idea that you soon won't be Mrs. Blake Chandler."

"That's true," Dina acknowledged. It was not an idea that could be implanted overnight.

The door to the library opened, and an older woman dressed in black was framed in its jamb. An indulgent smile curved her mouth as she spied the embracing pair. Dina stiffened for an instant in Chet's arms, then forced herself to relax.

"We've been wondering where the two of you had gone," the woman chided them. "It's time you came back to the party and received some of the toasts being made."

"We'll be there in a minute, Mother Chandler," Dina replied to the woman who was Blake's mother, her mother-in-law.

Norma Chandler was the epitome of a society matron, belonging to all the right garden clubs and fund-raising organizations for charity. Her role in life had always been the traditional one, centered around her home and family. With both husband and son dead, she clung to Dina as her family and to her home as security.

"If you don't, I'm afraid the party will move in here, and there's hardly enough room for them all." A hand touched the strands of pearls at her throat, the gesture indicating such a thing could never dare happen at one of her parties. The pearl-gray shade of her elegantly coiffed hair blended with the jewelry she wore.

"We'll be there in a minute, Mother Chandler," Chet added his promise to Dina's. With a nod the woman closed the door, and Chet glanced at Dina. "Do you suppose you'll be able to persuade her to wear something other than black to our wedding?"

"I doubt it." She moved out of his arms, a faintly cynical smile curving her lips. "Norma Chandler likes portraying the image of a tragic figure."

Within a few weeks after Dina's marriage to Blake, Kyle Chandler, his father, had died unexpectedly of a heart attack, and Norma Chandler had purchased an entire wardrobe of black. She had barely been out of mourning when they received news that Blake's plane was missing. Instantly Mrs. Chandler began dressing in black, not waiting for the notification that came a year ago declaring her son to be considered officially dead.

"She approves of our marriage. You know that, don't you?" Chet asked.

"Yes, she approves," Dina agreed, "for the sake of the company." And for the fact that there would only be one 'widow' Chandler instead of two—but Dina didn't say that, knowing it would sound small and unkind when her mother-in-law had been almost smothering in her love toward her.

"Mother Chandler still doesn't believe you're capable of running the company after all this time," Chet concluded from her response. He shook his head wryly.

"I couldn't do it without you." Dina stated it as a fact, not an expression of gratitude.

"I'm with you." He curved an arm around her waist as she started for the door to leave the room. "So you won't have to worry about that."

As Chet reached forward to open the door for her, Dina was reminded of that frozen instant when Norma Chandler had opened the door seconds ago. She wondered if the same thought had crossed her mother-in-law's mind as it had her own. She had recalled the numerous times Mrs. Chandler had opened the library door to find Dina sitting on Blake's lap locked in one of his crushing and possessive embraces. This time it had been Chet's arms that held her instead of Blake's. She wondered if her mother-in-law was as aware of the vast differences between the two men as she was.

In the last months, after the uncertainty of Blake's fate had been settled and there had been time to reflect, Dina had tried to imagine what the last two and a half years might have been like if

Blake had lived. Theirs had been such a brief, stormy marriage, carrying the portent of more years of the same, always with the possibility that one battle could have ended the union permanently.

Chet, on the other hand, was always predictable, and the time Dina spent with him was always pleasant. Under his supportive influence she had discovered skills and potentials she hadn't known she possessed. Her intelligence had been channeled into constructive fields and expanded to encompass more knowledge instead of being sharpened for warring exchanges with Blake.

Her personality had matured in a hurry, owing to the circumstances of Blake's disappearance. She had become a very confident and self-assured woman, and she gave all the credit for the change to Chet.

Some of her misgivings vanished as she walked out with Chet to rejoin the party in the main area of the house. There was no earthly reason not to enjoy the engagement party, none whatsoever.

The instant they returned to the spacious living room, they were engulfed by the sedate gathering of well-wishers. Each seemed to display a reverence for the antique furniture that abounded in the room, beautiful Victorian pieces enhanced by paintings and art objects. The atmosphere decreed formality and civil behavior.

"I see you found the two of them, Norma," Sam Lavecek announced belatedly. His voice had a tendency to boom, an abrasive sound that drew unnecessary attention to their absence from the party. "Off in some secluded corner, no doubt." He winked with faint suggestiveness at Dina. "Reminds me of the times you and Blake were always slipping away to cuddle in some corner." He glanced down at the brandy in his hand. "I miss that boy." It was an absent comment, his thoughts spoken aloud.

An awkward tension charged the moment. Chet, with his usual diplomacy, smoothed it over. "We all miss him, Sam," he asserted quietly, his arm curving protectively around Dina's shoulders.

"What?" Sam Lavecek's initial reaction was blankness, as if unaware that he said out loud what was on his mind. He flushed uncomfortably at the newly engaged pair. "Of course, we do, but it doesn't stop any of us from wishing you much happiness together," he insisted and lifted his glass, calling the others to a toast. "To Dina and Chet, and their future together."

Dina maintained her facade of smiling happiness, but it was an odd feeling to have the celebrants of their engagement party consist of Blake's family and friends. Without family herself, her parents having been killed in an automobile crash the year before she had met Blake, there had been no close relatives of her own to invite. What friends she had in Newport, she had met through Blake. Chet's family lived in Florida.

When Norma Chandler had asked to give them an engagement party, it had been a difficult offer to reject. Dina had chosen not to, finding it the easiest and quickest means to inform all of the Chandler relatives and friends of her decision to accept Chet's proposal. She wasn't blind to her mother-in-law's motives. Norma Chandler wished to remain close to

her. All her instincts were maternal, and Dina was
the only one left to mother.

But the engagement party had proved to be more
of a trial than Dina had thought. The announcement had raised too much inner restlessness and
vague doubts. None of the celebrants could see
that. She was too well schooled in concealing her
feelings. When the party ended at a suitable hour,
no one was the wiser. Not even Chet suspected that
she was still plagued by apprehensions when he
kissed her good night. It was something Dina knew
she would have to work out alone.

OVER THE WEEKEND, the news of their engagement
had filtered into the main office of the Chandler
hotel chain in Newport. Dina felt certain she had
spent the bulk of the morning confirming the
rumors that she was engaged to Chet.

She sincerely doubted that there was anyone in
the building who had not stopped at her office to
extend congratulations and questioning looks.

A mountain of work covered the massive walnut
desk top—letters to be answered, reports to be read
and memos to be issued. With her elbows on the
desk top, Dina rested her forehead on her hands,
rubbing the dull throb in its center. Her pale blond
hair had grown to the point where it could be pulled
to the nape of her neck in a neat bun, the style adding a few years to her relatively youthful appearance.

The clothing she wore to the office was chosen,
too, with an eye to detracting from her youth.
Today, it was a long-sleeved blouse of cream yellow

with a wine-colored vest and skirt, attractive and stylish yet professional-looking.

The intercom buzzed and Dina lifted her head, reaching over to press the button. "Yes?"

"Harry Landers is here to see you, Mrs. Chandler," was the reply from her secretary, Amy Wentworth—about the only one of the executive staff younger than Dina was.

"Send him in."

Dina picked up her reading glasses, which were lying on a stack of papers she had been reading, and put them on. She could see to read without them, but invariably after hours of reading the eye strain became too much. Lately she had taken to wearing them almost constantly at the office to avoid the headaches that accompanied the strain, and subconsciously because they added a business-like air to her appearance. There was a wry twist of her mouth as the doorknob to her office turned, an inner acknowledgement that she had been wrong in thinking everyone had been in to offer congratulations. Harry Landers hadn't, and the omission was about to be corrected. As the door opened, her mouth finished its curve into a polite smile of greeting.

"Good morning, Harry."

The tall and brawny white-haired man who entered smiled and returned the greeting. "Good morning, Mrs. Chandler." Only Chet used her Christian name at the office, and then only when they were alone. "I just heard the news that you and Chet are getting married. Congratulations," he offered predictably.

"Thank you," she nodded for what seemed like the hundredth time that morning.

There was no silent, unasked question in the look he gave her. "I'm truly glad for you, Mrs. Chandler. I know there are some people here who think you're somehow being unfaithful to Blake's memory by marrying again. Personally, I think it speaks well of your marriage to him."

"You do?" Her voice was briskly cool; she did not care for discussions about her private life, although her curiosity was rising by degrees as she tried to follow his logic.

"Yes—I mean, obviously your marriage to Blake was very satisfactory or you wouldn't want to enter the wedded state again," he reasoned.

"I see." Her smile was tight, lacking warmth. "Blake and I did have a good marriage." Whether they did, she couldn't say. It had been too brief. "And I know Chet and I will, too."

"When is the wedding?"

"We haven't set the date yet."

"Be sure to send me an invitation."

"We will." Dina's hopes for a quiet wedding and no reception were fast dissipating under the rush of requests to attend. An elopement was beginning to look inviting.

"At least you won't have to concern yourself with the company after you're married," Harry Landers observed with a benign smile.

"I beg your pardon?" Dina was instantly alert and on the defensive, no longer mouthing the polite words she had repeated all morning.

"After you're married, you can go back to being

a simple housewife. Chet will make a good president," he replied.

Why the accent on "simple," Dina wondered bitterly. "My marriage to Chet will have no effect on the company. It will continue to be run jointly by both of us with myself as president," she stated, not wanting to remember that the work had been done by Blake alone. Rigid with anger, she turned to the papers on her desk. "I don't see the monthly report from the Florida hotel. Has it come in?"

"I don't believe so." Her abrupt change of subject warned the man he was treading on forbidden ground. His previous open expression became closed and officious.

"Frank Miller is the manager there, isn't he?"

"Yes."

"Call him and find out where the report is. I want it on my desk by four this afternoon even if he has to telex it," she ordered.

"I'll see to it right away, Mrs. Chandler."

When the door closed behind him, Dina rose from the overstuffed cushion on her swivel office chair and walked to the window. Afterquakes of resentment were still trembling through her. Almost since Blake's disappearance, she had run the company with Chet's help; but her competence to fill the position still wasn't recognized by some of the executive officers.

It hadn't been by design but through necessity that she had taken over. When Blake disappeared over South America, the company had been like a ship without a rudder, without guidance or direction. It had operated smoothly for a while, then it began to flounder helplessly.

The key members of the executive staff, those who might have been competent enough to take over, had resigned to take positions with more solid companies, like rats deserting a sinking ship. That was when Dina had been forced to step in, by virtue of the Chandler name.

It hadn't been easy. The odds were stacked against her because she was young and a woman and totally ignorant of the machinations of the company, not to say limited in experience. Exerting her authority had been the most difficult part. Most of the staff were old enough to be her parents; and some, like Harry Landers, were old enough to be her grandparents.

Dina had learned the hard way, by trial and many errors. The worries, the fears that she had about Blake, she had to keep to herself. Very early she discovered that the men who offered her a shoulder to cry on were also insistently offering their beds.

More and more in those early days, she began turning to Chet for his unselfish and undemanding support. Not once did he make a single overture toward her, not until several months after Blake's death had been confirmed. She trusted him implicitly and he had never given her a reason to doubt him.

But Harry Landers had just put a question in her mind—one Dina didn't like facing, but there seemed to be no eluding it.

Shaking her head, Dina walked back to her desk. She picked up the telephone receiver and hesitated, staring at the numbers on the dial. There was a quick knock on her office door, followed by the click of the latch as it was opened without waiting for her permission to enter. Replacing the receiver, Dina turned to the door as Chet appeared.

"You'll never guess what I just heard," he whispered with exaggerated secrecy.

"What is it?" Dina grew tense.

"Chet Stanton is going to marry Mrs. Chandler."

What she expected him to say, Dina had no idea. But at his answer she laughed with a mixture of amusement and relief, some of her tension fleeing.

"You've heard that rumor, too, have you?" she retorted.

"Are you kidding?" He grimaced in a boyish fashion that made her heart warm to him all .the more. "I've been trying to get to my office since nine o'clock this morning and haven't made it yet. I keep getting stopped along the way."

"As bad as that?" Dina smiled.

"The hallway is a veritable gauntlet."

She knew the feeling. "We should have called everybody together this morning, made the announcement, then gone to work. It would have made a more productive morning."

"Hindsight, my love," he chided, walking over to kiss her lightly on the cheek.

"Yes," Dina agreed. She removed her glasses and made a show of concentrating on them as she placed them on the desk top. "Now that everyone knows, they're all waiting for me to hand in my resignation and name you as. the successor to the Chandler throne." Without seeming to, she watched Chet's reaction closely.

"I hope you set them straight about that," he replied without hesitation. "We make an excellent team. And there certainly isn't any reason to break up a winning combination in the company just because we're getting married."

"That's what I thought," she agreed.

Taking her by the shoulders, Chet turned her to face him, tipping his head to one side in an inquiring manner. "Have I told you this morning how beautiful you are?"

"No." The edges of her mouth dimpled slightly as she answered him in the same serious tone that he had used. "But you can tell me now."

"You're very beautiful, darling."

With the slightest pressure, he drew her yielding shape to him. As his mouth lightly took possession of hers, the intercom buzzed. Dina moved out of his arms with a rueful smile of apology.

She pressed the button. "Yes, Amy?"

"Jacob Stone is on line one," came the reply.

"Thank you." Dina broke the connection and glanced at Chet with a resigned shrug of her shoulders.

"Jake Stone," he repeated. "That's the Chandler family attorney, isn't it?"

"Yes," she nodded, reaching for the telephone. "Probably some business to do with Blake's estate."

"That's my cue for an exit." And Chet started for the door.

"Dinner tonight at eight?" Dina questioned.

"Perfect," he agreed with a wink.

"Call Mother Chandler and tell her I've invited you." She picked up the telephone receiver, her finger hovering above the blinking button on line one.

"Consider it done."

Dina watched him leave. Just for a few minutes, Harry Landers had made her suspect that Chet might be marrying her to elevate his position in the company. But his instant and casual rejection of the suggestion of becoming president had erased that. Her trust in him was once again complete.

She pushed the button. "Hello, Mr. Stone. Dina Chandler speaking."

"Ah, Mrs. Chandler. How are you?" came the gravelly voice in answer.

"Just fine, thank you."

CHAPTER TWO

By THE END of the week, the excitement generated by the news of their engagement had died down and work was able to settle into a routine again. The invisible pressure the news had evoked eased as well.

Yet on Saturday morning Dina wakened with the sun, unable to go back to sleep. Finally she stopped trying, arose and dressed in slacks and white blouse with a pullover sweater. The other members of the household, Blake's mother and their housekeeper, Deirdre, were still asleep.

Dina hurriedly tidied the room, unfolding the blue satin coverlet from the foot of the four-poster bed and smoothing it over the mattress. Deirdre was such a perfectionist that she would probably do it over again. Fluffing the satin pillow shams, Dina placed them at the head of the bed.

The clothes she had worn last night were lying on the blue and gold brocade cushion of the love seat. Dina hung them up in the large closet. The neckscarf she folded and carried to its drawer.

Inside, the gilt edge of a picture frame gleamed amidst the lingerie and fashion accessories. It lay face down, concealing the photograph of Blake. Until Chet had given her an engagement ring, the picture had been on the bedside table, Now it was relegated to a dresser drawer, a photograph of the past that had nothing to do with the present. Dina closed the drawer and glanced around the room. Everything seemed to be in order.

After Blake's disappearance two and a half years ago, it had seemed senseless for both Dina and his mother to keep separate households, especially when the days began to stretch into weeks and months. In the end Dina had sublet the apartment she and Blake had in town to move to the suburbs with his mother.

She had thought it would ease her loneliness and provide an outlet for her inner fears, but it hadn't proved to be so. Dina had spent the bulk of her private time consoling Mother Chandler, as she called her mother-in-law, and had received little if any consolation in return.

Still, it was a suitable arrangement, a place to sleep and eat, with all the housekeeping and meals done by others. With most of her time and energy spent in keeping the company going, the arrangement had become a definite asset.

Now, as she tiptoed out of the house into the dawn, Dina wished for the privacy of her own home, where she could steal into the kitchen and fix an early morning breakfast without feeling she was invading someone else's turf. And Deirdre was jealously possessive about her kitchen.

Closing the door, she listened for the click of the lock. When she heard it, she turned to the steps leading to the driveway and the white Porsche parked there. Inside the house the telephone rang, loud in the silence of the pink morning.

Dina stopped and began rummaging through her oversize purse for the house key. It was seldom used since there was always someone to let her in. Before she found it, the phone had stopped ringing. She waited several seconds to see if it would start ringing again. Someone in the house must have answered it, Dina decided, or else the party must have decided to call later in the morning.

Skimming down the steps, she hurried to the Porsche, folding the top down before climbing in and starting the engine. With doughnuts and coffee in a Styrofoam container from a pastry shop, she drove through the quiet business streets.

There was a salty tang to the breeze ruffling her hair. Dina shook her head to let its cool fingers rake through the silken gold strands. Her blue eyes narrowed in decision as she turned the sports car away from the street that would take her to the office building and headed toward the solitude of an early morning ocean beach.

Sitting on a piece of driftwood, Dina watched the sun finish rising on Rhode Island Sound, the water shimmering and sparkling as the waves lapped the long strand of ocean beach. The city of Newport was located on the island of Rhode Island, from which the state derived its name.

The doughnut crumbs had been tossed to the sea-gulls, still swooping and soaring nearby in case she had missed one. It was peaceful and quiet. The nearest person was a surf fisherman, a stick figure distantly visible. It was one of those times when she thought of many things as she sat, but couldn't remember a single one when she rose to leave.

It was nine o'clock, the time she usually arrived at the office for a half-day's work, minimum. But Dina couldn't think of a single item that was pressing, except the one the family attorney had called about the first of the week.

Returning to her Porsche parked off the road near the beach, she drove to the nearest telephone booth and stopped. She rummaged through her purse for change and dialed the office number. It was answered on the second ring.

"Amy? This is Mrs. Chandler." She shut the door of the phone booth to close out the whine of the semitrailer going by. "I won't be in this morning, but there's some correspondence on the dictaphone I would like typed this morning."

"I've already started it," her young secretary answered.

"Good. When you have it done, leave it on my desk. Then you can call it a day. All right?"

"Yes, thank you, Mrs. Chandler." Amy Wentworth was obviously delighted.

"See you Monday," Dina said, and hung up.

Back in the white sports car, she headed for the boat marina where Blake's sailboat was docked. She parked the car by the small shed that served as an office. A man sat in a chair out front.

Balanced was the better word, as the chair was tilted back, allowing only the two rear legs to support it. The man's arms were folded in front of him and a faded captain's hat was pulled over his face, permitting only a glimpse of his double chin and the graying stubble of beard.

Dina hopped out of the sports car, smiling at the

man who hadn't changed in almost three years. "Good morning, Cap'n Tate."

She waited for his slow, drawling New England voice to return the greeting. He was a character and he enjoyed being one.

The chair came down with a thump as a large hand pushed the hat back on top of his head. Gray eyes stared at her blankly for a minute before recognition flickered in them.

"How do, Miz Chandler." He rose lumberingly to his feet, pulling his faded trousers up to cover his paunch. The end result was to accentuate it.

"It's been so long since I've seen you. How have you been?"

"Mighty fine, Miz Chandler, mighty fine." The owner of the marina smiled and succeeded in extending the smile to his jowled cheeks. "I s'pose you're here to get the *Starfish* cleaned out. Shore was sorry when your attorney told me you was goin' to rent it out."

"Yes, I know." Her smile faded slightly. Getting rid of the boat seemed to be like closing the final chapter about Blake in her life. "But it was pointless to keep the boat dry-docked here, unused."

"She's a damn fine boat," he insisted, puffing a bit as he stepped inside the shed door and reached for a key. "Never know, someday you might want it yourself."

Dina laughed, a little huskily. "You know I'm not a sailor, Cap'n Tate. I need a whole bottle of motion-sickness pills just to make it out of the harbor without getting seasick!"

"Then you sleep the whole time." He guffawed

and started coughing. "I never will forget that time Blake came carrying you off the boat sound asleep. He told me aft'wards that you didn't wake up till the next morning."

"If you will recall, that was the last time he even suggested I go sailing with him." She took the key he handed her, feeling a poignant rush of memories and trying to push them back.

"D'ya want some help movin' any of that stuff?" he offered.

"No, thank you." She couldn't imagine the two of them in the small cabin, not with Cap'n Tate's protruding belly. "I can manage."

"You just give me a holler if you need anything," he said nodding his grizzled head. "You know where she's docked."

"I do." With a wave of her hand, Dina started down the long stretch of dock.

Masts, long, short and medium, stood in broken lines along the pier, sails furled, the hulls motionless in the quiet water. Her steps were directed by memory along the boards. Although she had rarely ever joined Blake after her first two disastrous attempts at sailing, Dina had often come to the marina to wait for his return. But Blake wouldn't be coming back anymore.

The bold letters of the name *Starfish* stood out clearly against the white hull. Dina paused, feeling the tightness in her throat. Then, scolding herself, she stepped aboard. The wooden deck was dull, no longer gleaming and polished as Blake had kept it.

It didn't do any good to tell herself she shouldn't have waited so long to do something about the boat. There had been so many other decisions to make and demands on her time. Plus there had been so many legal entanglements surrounding Blake's disappearance. Those had become knots at the notification of his death. Since his estate wasn't settled, the boat still couldn't be sold until the court decreed the dispensation of his property.

The *Starfish* had been dry-docked since his disappearance, everything aboard exactly the way he had left it after his last sail. Dina unlocked the cabin to go below. The time had come to pack away all his things. Jake Stone, the family attorney, had decided the boat should be leased, even if it couldn't be sold yet, to eliminate the maintenance costs and to keep it from deteriorating through lack of use.

It had occurred to Dina that she could have arranged for someone else to clear away his things and clean up the boat. That was what she planned to do when the attorney had phoned the first of the week to tell her he had received the court's permission to lease the boat. But she was here now and the task lay ahead of her.

Opening drawers and doors, she realized there was a great deal more aboard than she had supposed. The storehouse of canned goods in the cupboards would have brought a smile of delight to any gourmet, but Blake had always been very particular about his food and the way it was prepared. Sighing, Dina wondered how many of the cans were still good. What a waste it would be if she had to throw them all out.

Picking up a can, she quickly set it down. The first order was to get a general idea of what had to be done. She continued her methodical examination of the cabin's contents. The clean, if now musty, clothes brought a smile to her lips. It was funny how a person's memory of little things could dim over such a short time as a few years.

A glance at his clothes brought it all back. Blake had been very meticulous about his clothes, being always clean and well dressed. Even the several changes of denim Levi's kept aboard the boat were creased and pressed. A thin coating of dust couldn't hide the snow-white of his sneakers.

Both seemed something of an extreme, yet Dina couldn't remember a time when she had seem him dressed in a manner that could be described as carelessly casual. It made him sound a bit pompous, but the trait hadn't been at all abrasive.

Blake had been used to good things all his life—a beautiful home, excellent food, vintage wines and specially tailored clothes. Spoiled? With a trace of arrogance? Perhaps, Dina conceded. He had been something of a playboy when she had met him, with devastating charm when he wanted to turn it on. Brilliantly intelligent and almost dreadfully organized, he had been exciting and difficult to live with.

Not at all like Chet, she concluded again. But what was the point in comparing? What could be gained by holding up Blake's smooth sophistication to Chet's easygoing nature? With a shrug of confusion, she turned away from the clothes, shutting her mind to the unanswerable questions.

For the better part of the day she worked aboard the boat, first packing and carrying Blake's belongings to the Porsche, where she stuffed them in every conceivable corner of the small sports car. Then she began cleaning away the years of dust and salt spray, airing the mattresses and cushions, and polishing the interior woodwork.

Dirty and sweaty and physically exhausted, she returned the key to the crusty marina operator. Yet the laborious job had been cathartic, leaving her with an oddly refreshed feeling. Lately all her energy had been expended mentally. The hard work felt good even if her muscles would be stiff and sore tomorrow.

She was humming to herself as the white Porsche rounded the corner onto the street where she lived with her mother-in-law. Ahead was the Chandler home, an imposing brick structure that towered two and a half stories into the air. It was set back from the road by a formal lawn dotted with perfectly shaped trees and well-cut shrubs and a scattering of flower beds. The many windows and double entrance doors were a pristine shade of ivory. At the sight of the half dozen cars parked around the cul-de-sac of the driveway, Dina frowned and slowed the car, forced to park it some distance from the entrance.

There wasn't any dinner party she had forgotten, was there, she wondered to herself. The cars resembled those belonging to close family friends. One, the silver gray Cadillac, was Chet's. She glanced at her watch. He had said he would stop around seven for a drink before taking her out to dinner. It was barely five o'clock.

Her mouth formed a disgruntled line. She had hoped to soak in a tubful of scented bubbles for an hour, but obviously that luxury was going to be denied her. And why hadn't Mother Chandler mentioned she would be entertaining this evening? It wasn't like her.

Puzzled, Dina raised the convertible top of her sports car and rolled up the windows. This was not the time to transport all the items from the car into the house, so she climbed out of the car, her handbag slung over her shoulder, and locked the doors.

Happy voices were talking all over each other from the living room as she entered the house. The double doors of carved oak leading into the room were closed, concealing the owners of the voices. The foyer, with its richly grained oak woodwork complementing pale yellow walls, was empty. The wide staircase rising to the second floor beckoned, its gold carpeted treads like sunlight showing her the path, the carved oak balustrade catching the reflected color. She hesitated, then decided to go for a quick wash and change while her return was still unnoticed.

Only it wasn't unnoticed. As she started to cross the foyer for the stairs leading to the second floor and her bedroom, one of the double doors was surreptitiously opened. Her eyes widened as Chet slipped out, his handsome features strained and tense.

"Where have you been?" There was a hint of desperation in his voice.

If it weren't for the joyful tone of the voices in the other room, Dina might have guessed that some catastrophe had befallen them, judging by Chet's expression.

"At the marina," she answered.

"The marina?" he repeated in disbelief. Again there was that strangled tightness in his voice. "My God, I've been calling all over trying to find you. I never even considered the marina. What were you doing there, for heaven's sake?"

"The *Sarfish*—the boat has been leased. I was getting it cleaned up." The explanation was made while Dina tried to think what crisis could have arisen that Chet would have so urgently needed to contact her about.

"Of all the times—"

Dina broke in sharply. "What's going on?" His attitude was too confusing when she couldn't fathom the reason for it.

"Look, there's something I have to tell you." Chet moistened his lips nervously, his gray blue gaze darting over her face as if trying to judge something from her expression. "But I don't know how to say it."

"What is it?" she demanded impatiently. His tension was becoming contagious.

He took her by the shoulders, his expression deadly serious as he gazed intently into her eyes. Her muscles were becoming sore and they protested at the tightness of his hold.

"It's this . . ." he began earnestly.

But he got no further as a low, huskily pitched male voice interrupted. "Chet seems to think you're going to go into a state of shock when you find out I'm alive."

The floor rocked beneath her feet. Dina managed a half turn on her treacherously unsteady footing, magnetically drawn to the voice. The whole floor seemed to give way when she saw its owner, yet she remained upright, her collapsing muscles supported by Chet.

There was a dreamlike unreality to the moment.

Almost nightmarelike, since it seemed a cruel joke for someone to stand in the doorway of the living room masquerading as Blake, mimicking his voice.

She stared wordlessly at the tall figure framed by the living-room doors. There was much about the chiseled features that resembled Blake—the wide forehead, the carved cheek and jaw, the strong chin and classically straight nose.

Yet there were differences, too. The sun had burned this man's face a dusky tan, making it leathery and tough, giving a hardness to features that in Blake had been suavely handsome. The eyes were the same dark brown, but they wore a narrowed, hooded look as they seemed to pierce into the very marrow of her soul .

His hair was the same deep shade of umber brown, but its waving thickness was much longer than Blake had ever worn it, giving the impression of being rumpled instead of smoothly in place. As tall as Blake, this man's build was more muscled. Not that Blake had been a weakling by any means; it was just that this man seemed more developed without appearing heavier.

The differences registered with computer swiftness, her brain working while the rest of her was reeling from the similarities. The buzzing in her head continued nonstop, facts clicking into place.

But it wasn't her eyes that Dina trusted. What

finally led her to a conclusion was Chet's peculiar behavior before this man appeared; his innate kindness, which would never have permitted a cruel joke like this to be played on her; and the something that he was going to tell before they were interrupted.

Blake was alive. And he was standing in the doorway. She swayed forward, but her feet wouldn't move. Chet's hands tightened in support and she turned her stunned gaze to him. The confirmation was there in his carefully watchful face.

"It's true," she breathed, neither a statement nor a question.

Chet nodded, a silent warning in his eyes. It was then that Dina felt the cold weight of his engagement ring around her finger, and the blood drained from her face. Her hands reached out to cling to Chet's arms, suddenly and desperately needing his support to remain upright.

"It seems Chet was right," that familiar, lazy voice drawled in an arid tone. "My return is more of a shock to you than I thought it would be," Blake observed. The angle of his head shifted slightly to the side to direct his next words over his shoulder without releasing Dina from his level gaze. "She needs some hot, sweet coffee, laced with a stiff shot of brandy."

"Exactly," Chet agreed, and curved a bracing arm around her waist. "Let's find you a place to sit down, Dina." Numbly she accepted his help, aware of his gaze flickering to Blake. "Seeing you standing in the doorway was bound to have been like seeing a ghost. I told you we were all convinced you were dead."

"Not me," Mother Chandler contradicted him, moving to stand beside her son. "I always knew somehow that he was still alive somewhere out there, despite what everyone said."

Fleetingly, Dina was aware of the blatant lie in her mother-in-law's assertion. The thought had barely formed when she realized there were others in the living room. She recognized the faces of close family friends, gathered to celebrate Blake's return. They had been watching the reunion between husband and wife—or rather, the lack of it.

In that paralyzing second, Dina realized she had not so much as touched Blake, let alone joyously fallen into his arms. Her one swaying attempt had been accidentally checked by Chet's steadying hold. It would seem staged and faked if she did so now.

Equally startling was the discovery that she would have to fake it because, although the man in front of her was obviously Blake Chandler, he did not seem like the same man she had married. She felt as if she were looking at a total stranger. He knew what she was thinking and feeling; she could see it in the coolness of his expression, aloof and chilling.

As she and Chet approached the doorway, Blake stepped to one side, giving them room. He smiled down at his mother, his expression revealing nothing to the others that might let them think he found her behavior unnatural under the circumstances.

"If you were so positive I was alive, mother, why are you wearing black?" he chided her.

Color rose in Norma Chandler's cheeks. "For your father, Blake," she responded, not at a loss for an explanation.

Everyone was still standing, watching, as Chet guided Dina to the empty cushions of the sofa. After she was seated, he automatically sat down beside her. Blake had followed them into the room.

Every nerve in Dina's body was aware of his presence, although she wasn't able to lift her gaze to him. Guilt burned inside her, gnawing away at any spontaneous reaction she might have had. It didn't help when Blake sat down in the armchair nearest her end of the couch.

The housekeeper appeared, setting a china cup and saucer on the glass-topped table in front of the sofa. "Here's your coffee, just the way Mr. Blake ordered it."

"Thank you, Deirdre," she murmured. She reached for the china cup filled with steaming dark liquid, but her hands were shaking like aspen leaves and she couldn't hold on to it.

Out of the corner of her eye, she caught a suggestion of movement from Blake, as if he was about to lean forward to help her. Chet's hand was already there, lifting the cup to carry it to her lips. It was purely an automatic reaction on Chet's part. He had become used to doing things for her in the past two and a half years, just as Dina had become used to having him do them.

Instinctively, she knew he hadn't told Blake of their engagement and she doubted if anyone else had. But Chet's solicitous concern was telling its own story. And behind that facade of lazy interest, Blake was absorbing every damning detail. Without knowing it, Chet was making matters worse.

The hot and sweetly potent liquid Dina sipped

eased the constriction strangling her voice, and she found the strength to raise her hesitant gaze to Blake's.

"How . . ." she began self-consciously. "I mean when...."

"I walked out of the jungle two weeks ago." He anticipated her question and answered it.

"Two weeks ago?" That was before she had agreed to marry Chet. "Why didn't you let . . . someone know?"

"It was difficult to convince the authorities that I was who I claimed to be. They, too, believed I was dead." There was a slashing line to his mouth, a cynical smile. "It must have been easier for Lazarus back in the Biblical days to return from the dead."

"Are you positive I can't fix you a drink, Mr. Blake?" the housekeeper inquired. "A martini?"

"Nothing, thank you."

Dina frowned. In the past Blake had always drunk two, if not three martinis before dinner. She had not been wrong. There were more than just surface changes in him during the last two and a half years. Unconsciously she covered her hand with her right, hiding not only the wedding rings Blake had given her, but Chet's engagement ring, as well.

"The instant they believed Blake's story," his mother inserted to carry on his explanation, "he caught the first plane out to come home." She beamed at him like the adoring and doting mother that she was.

"You should have phoned." Dina couldn't help saying it. Forewarned, she might have been better prepared for the new Blake Chandler.

"I did."

Simultaneously as he spoke, Dina remembered the telephone ringing in the dawn hour as she had left the house. Seconds. She had missed knowing about his return by seconds.

"I'd switched off my extension," Norma Chandler said, "and Deidre was wearing her earplugs. Did you hear it, Dina?"

"No. No, I'd already left," answered Dina.

"When Blake didn't get any answer here," Chet continued the story, "he called me."

"Chet was as stunned as you were, Dina," Blake smiled, but Dina suspected that she was the only one who noticed the lack of amusement in his voice. She knew her gaze wavered under the keenness of his.

"I came over right away to let you and Mrs. Chandler know," Chet finished.

"Where were you, Dina?" Sam Lavecek grumped. He was Blake's godfather and a very old friend of both Blake's mother and father. Over the years he had become something of a Dutch uncle to Blake, later extending the relationship to Dina. "Chet has been half out of his mind worrying about where you were all day. Played hooky from the office, did you?"

"I was at the marina," she answered, and turned to Blake. "The *Starfish* has been leased to a couple, and they plan to sail to Florida for the winter. I spent the day cleaning it up and moving out all of your things."

"What a pity, boy!" Sam Lavecek sympathized, slapping the arm of his chair. "You always did love going out on that boat. Now, the very day you come home, it's being turned over to someone else."

"It's only a boat, Sam." There was an enigmatic darkness to his eyes that made his true thoughts impossible to see.

To Dina, in her supersensitive state, he seemed to be implying something else. Perhaps he didn't object to his boat being loaned to someone else—as long as it wasn't his wife. Her apprehension mounted.

"You're right!" the older man agreed with another emphatic slap of his hand on the armchair. "It's only a boat. And what's that compared to having you back? It's a miracle! A miracle!"

The statement brought a surfeit of questions for Blake to answer about the crash and the events that followed. Dina listened to his narrative. Each word that came from his mouth made him seem more and more a stranger.

The small chartered plane had developed engine trouble and had crashed in the teeming jungle. When Blake had come to, the other four people aboard were dead and he was trapped in the twisted wreckage with a broken leg and a few broken ribs. There had been a deep gash on his forehead, still seeping blood, and other cuts and bruises. Dina's gaze found the scar that had made a permanent crease in his forehead.

Blake didn't go into too much detail about how he had got out of the plane the following day, but Dina had a vivid imagination and pictured the agony he must have endured fighting his way out with his injuries, letting the wreckage become a coffin for the mangled lifeless bodies of the others. Not knowing when or if he would be rescued, Blake had been forced to set his own leg.

That was something Dina could not visualize him doing. In the past, when there was anything that required professional skill or experience, Blake had always hired someone to do it. So for him to set his own broken bone, regardless of the dire circumstances, seemed completely out of character, something the man she had known would never have done.

When the emergency supply of rations from the plane had run out, Blake had foraged for his food, his diet consisting of fruits and whatever wild animals he could trap, catch or kill. And this was supposed to be the same Blake Chandler who had considered the killing of wild game a disgusting sport and who dined on gourmet cuisine.

Blake, who despised flies and mosquitoes, told of the insects that swarmed in the jungle, flying, crawling, biting, stinging, until he no longer noticed them. The heat and humidity of the jungle rotted his shoes and clothes, forcing him to improvise articles of clothing from the skins of the animals he had killed. Blake, the meticulous dresser, always presenting such a well-groomed appearance....

As he began his tale of the more than two-year-long walk out of the jungle, Dina discovered the crux of the difference. Blake had left Rhode Island a civilized man and had come back part primitive. She stared at him with seeing eyes.

Leaning back in his chair, he looked indolent and relaxed, yet Dina knew his muscles were like coiled springs, always ready to react with the swiftness of a predatory animal. His senses, his nerves were alert to everything going on around him. Nothing escaped the notice of that hooded dark gaze. From the lurking depths of those hard brown eyes, Blake seemed to be viewing them all with cynical amusement, as if he found the so-called dangers and problems of their civilized world laughable when compared to the battle of survival he had fought and won.

"There's something I don't understand," Sam Lavecek commented, frowning when Blake had completed his basically sketchy narrative. "Why did the authorities tell us you were dead after they'd found the wreckage? Surely they must have discovered there was a body missing," he added bluntly.

"I don't imagine they did," Blake answered in a calm, matter-of-fact tone.

"Did you bury their bodies, Blake?" his mother asked. "Is that why they didn't find them?"

"No, mother, I didn't." The cynical amusement that Dina suspected he felt was there, glittering through the brown shutters of the indulgent look he gave his mother. "It would have taken a bulldozer to carve out a grave in that tangled mess of brush, trees and roots. I had no choice but to leave them in the plane. Unfortunately, the jungle is filled with scavengers."

Dina blanched. He sounded so cold and insensitive! Blake had been a passionately vital and volatile man, quick to fly into a temper and quick to love.

What had he become? How much would the savagery in his life in the last two and a half years influence his future? Would his determination become ruthlessness? Would his innate leadership become tyranny? Would his compassion for others become contempt? Would his love turn to lust? Was he a virile man or a male animal? He was her husband, and Dina shuddered at what the answers to those questions might be.

Distantly she heard the housekeeper enter the room to inquire, "What time would you like dinner served this evening, Mrs. Chandler?"

There was hesitation before Norma Chandler replied, "In about an hour, Deirdre. That will be all right for everyone, won't it?" and received a murmur of agreement.

From the sofa cushions beside her, Chet expanded on his agreement to remark, "That will give you ample time to freshen up before dinner, won't it, Dina?"

She clutched at the lifeline he had unknowingly tossed her. "Yes, it will." She wanted desperately to be alone for a few minutes to sort through her jumbled thoughts, terribly afraid she was overreacting. Rising, she addressed her words to everyone. "Please excuse me. I won't be long."

Dina had the disquieting sensation of Blake's eyes following her as she walked from the room. But he made no attempt to stop her, nor offer to come with her to share a few minutes alone, much to her relief.

CHAPTER THREE

THE BRIEF SHOWER had washed away the last lingering traces of unreality. Wrapping the sash to her royal blue terry-cloth robe around her middle, Dina walked through the open doorway of the private bath to her bedroom. She moved to the clothes closet at the far corner of the room to choose what she would wear for dinner, all the while trying to assure herself that she was making mountains out of molehills where Blake was concerned.

There was a click, and then movement in her peripheral vision. She turned as the door opened and Blake walked in. Her mouth opened to order out the intruder, then closed. He was her husband. How could she order him out of her bedroom?

His gaze swept the room, located her, and stopped, fixing her with a stare like a predator would his prey. Her fingers clasped the folds of her robe at the throat, her palms moistening with nervous perspiration. Dina was conscious of the implied intimacy of the room and her own nakedness beneath the terry-cloth material. Blood pounded in her head like a thousand jungle drums signaling danger. Vulnerable, she was wary of him.

The brand-new tan suit and tie he wore gave him a cultured look, but she wasn't taken in by the thin veneer of refinement. It didn't conceal the latent power of that muscled physique, nor soften the rough edges of his sun-hardened features. Blake closed the door, not releasing her from his pinning gaze, and searing alarm halted her breath.

"I've come through hell to get back to you, Dina, yet you can't seem to walk across a room to meet me." The accusation was made in a smooth, low tone rife with sardonic amusement.

His words prodded her into movement. Too much time had elapsed since his return for her to rush into his arms. Her steps were stiff, her back rigid as she approached him. She was cautious of him and it showed. Even if she wanted to, she doubted if she could batter down the wall of reserve she had erected. Stopping in front of him, she searched her mind for welcoming words that she could issue sincerely.

"I'm glad you came back safely," were the ones she could offer that had the ring of truth.

Blake waited . . . for her kiss. The muscles in her stomach contracted sharply with the realization. After a second's hesitation, she forced herself on tiptoe to bring her lips against his mouth in a cool kiss. His large hands spanned the back of her waist, their imprint burning through the material onto her naked flesh. His light touch didn't seem at all familiar. It was almost alien.

At her first attempt to end the kiss, his arms became a vise, fingers raking into her silver gold hair to force her lips to his. Her slender curves were pressed against the hard contours of his body. Her heartbeat skittered madly, then accelerated in alarm.

The hungry demand of his bruising mouth asked more than Dina could give to a man who seemed more of a stranger than her husband. She struggled to free herself of his iron hold and was surprised when Blake let her twist away.

Her breathing was rapid and uneven as she avoided his eyes. "I have to get dressed." She pretended that was her reason for rejecting his embrace. "The others are waiting downstairs."

Those fathomless brown eyes were boring holes into her. Dina could feel them even as she turned away to retrace her steps to the closet and her much-needed clothes. Her knees felt watery.

"You mean Chet is waiting," Blake corrected her with deadly softness.

Her blood ran cold. "Of course. Isn't Chet there with the others?" She feigned ignorance of his meaning and immediately regretted not taking advantage of the opening he had given her to tell him about Chet.

"I've had two and a half years of forced celibacy, Dina. How about you?" The dry contempt in his question spun her around, blue fires of indignation flashing in her eyes, but Blake didn't give her a chance to defend her honor. "How long was it after I disappeared before Chet moved in?"

"He did not move in!" she flashed.

With the swiftness of a swooping hawk, he seized her left hand. His savage grip almost crushed the slender bones of her fingers into a pulp, drawing a gasp of pain from her.

"Figuratively speaking!" His mouth was a thin, cruel line as he lifted her hand. "Or don't you call it

moving in when another man's ring joins the ones I
put on your finger? Did you think I wouldn't see
it?" he blazed. "Did you think I wouldn't notice the
looks the two of you were exchanging and the way
all the others watched the three of us?" He released
her hand in a violent gesture of disgust. Dina
nursed the pain-numbed fingers, cradling them in
her right hand. "And neither of you had the guts to
tell me!"

"Neither of us really had a chance," she
responded defensively, her temper flaring from the
flame of his. "It isn't an announcement one wants
to make in front of others. What was I supposed to
say when I saw you standing in the doorway, a husband I thought was dead? 'Darling, I'm so glad
you're alive. Oh, by the way, I'm engaged to
another man.' Please credit me for having a bit
more delicacy than that!"

He gave her a long, hard look. His anger was so
tightly controlled that it almost frightened her. It
was like looking at a capped volcano, knowing that
inside it was erupting, and wondering when the lid
would blow.

"This is some homecoming," Blake declared in a
contemptuous breath. "A wife who wishes I were
still in the grave!"

"I don't wish that," she denied.

"This engagement—" he began, bitter sarcasm
coating his words.

"The way you say it makes it sound like something sordid," Dina protested, "and it isn't. Chet
and I have been engaged for barely more than a
week. At the time that he proposed to me, I thought
you were dead and I was free to accept."

"Now you know differently. I'm alive. You're my wife, not my widow. You're still married to me." The way he said it, in such cold, concise tones, made it sound like a life sentence.

Dina was trembling and she didn't know why. "I'm aware of that, Blake." Her voice was taut to keep out the tremors. "But this isn't the time to discuss the situation. Your mother is waiting dinner and I still have to get dressed."

For a few harrowing seconds, she thought he was going to argue. "Yes," he agreed slowly, "this isn't the time."

She heard the door being yanked open and flinched as it was slammed shut. If this was a new beginning for their marriage, it was off to a rotten start. They had argued before Blake had disappeared, and now war had nearly been declared on his return. Dina shuddered and walked to the closet again.

Her arrival downstairs coincided with Deirdre's announcement that dinner would be served. Blake was there to escort her into the formal dining room. A chandelier of cut crystal and polished brass hung above the table, glittering down on the Irish linen tablecloth set with the best of his mother's silver and china. An elaborate floral arrangement sat in the center of the buffet, not too near the table so its scent would not interfere with the aroma of the food. Blake was being warmly welcomed home, by everyone but her, and Dina was painfully conscious of the fact.

As they all took their chairs around the Danish styled dining table, the tension in the air was almost electrical. Yet Dina seemed to be the only one who noticed it. Blake sat at the head of the table, the place of honor, with his mother at the opposite end and Chet seated on her right. Dina sat on Blake's left.

Ever since she had come down, Blake had possessively kept her at his side, as if showing everyone that she was his and effectively separating her from Chet. On the surface, he seemed all smiles, at times giving her glimpses of his former devastating charm. But there was still anger smoldering in his brown eyes whenever his gaze was directed to her.

When everyone was seated, the housekeeper came in carrying a tureen of soup. "I fixed your favorite, Mr. Blake," she announced, a beaming smile on her square-jawed face. "Cream of asparagus."

"Bless you, Deidre." He smiled broadly. "Now that's the way to welcome a man home!"

The sharp side of his double-edged remark sliced at Dina. She paled at the censure, but otherwise retained a firm hold on her poise.

The meal was an epicurean's delight, from the soup to the lobster thermidor to the ambrosia of fresh fruit. Blake made all the right comments and compliments, but Dina noticed he didn't seem to savor the taste of the various dishes the way she remembered he had in the past. She had the impression that dining had been reduced to the simple matter of eating. Food was food however it was prepared, and man needed food to live.

Coffee was served in the living room so Deirdre could clear away the dishes. Again Dina was kept at

Blake's elbow. Chet was on the far side of the room. As she glanced his way, he looked up, smoke blue eyes meeting the clear blue of hers. He murmured a quick excuse to the older woman who had him cornered—a Mrs. Burnside, an old school friend of Norma Chandler—and made his way toward her.

Through the cover of her lashes, Dina dared a glance at Blake and saw the faint narrowing of his gaze as Chet approached. The smile on Chet's face was strained when he stopped in front of them. Dina guessed he was trying to find a way to tell Blake of their engagement and she wished there was a way to let him know that Blake was aware of it.

"It seems like old times, Blake," Chet began, forcing a camaraderie into his voice, "coming over to your house for dinner and seeing you and . . . ." His gaze slid nervously to Dina.

"Chet," Blake interrupted calmly, "Dina has told me about your engagement."

The room grew so quiet Dina was certain a feather could have been heard dropping on the carpet. All eyes were focused on the trio, as if a brilliant spotlight were shining on them. She discovered that, like everyone else, she was holding her breath. After the savage anger Blake had displayed upstairs, she wasn't sure what might happen next.

"I'm glad you know. I . . . ." Chet lowered his gaze searching for words.

Blake filled in the moment's pause. "I want you to know I don't bear any ill feelings. You've always been a good friend and I'd like it to continue that way." Dina started to sigh with relief. "After all, what are friends for?"

No one except Dina seemed to pay any attention to the last caustic comment. Chet was too busy shaking the hand Blake offered in friendship. The others were murmuring among themselves about the moment for which they had been waiting all day.

"Naturally the engagement is broken," Blake joked with a smile that contrasted with the sharply serious light in his eyes.

"Naturally," Chet agreed with an answering smile.

And Dina felt a rush of anger that she could be tossed aside so readily without protest. For that matter, she hadn't even been consulted about her wishes.

Immediately she berated herself. It was what she wanted. Blake was alive and she was married to him. She didn't want to divorce him to marry Chet, so why was she fussing? A simple matter of ego, she decided.

After the confrontation over the engagement, the party became anticlimactic. There was a steady trickle of departures among the guests. One minute Dina was wishing Mrs. Burnside goodbye and the next she was alone in the foyer with Blake, his eyes watching her in that steady, measured way she found so unnerving.

"That's the last of them," he announced.

Dina glanced around. "Where's your mother?"

"In the living room helping Deirdre clean up."

"I'll give them a hand." She started to turn away.

But Blake caught her arm. "There's no need." He released it as quickly as he had captured it. "They can handle it by themselves."

Dina didn't protest. The day had been unconscionably long and she felt enervated from the physical and mental stress she had experienced. What she really wanted was a long night of hard, dreamless sleep. She started for the stairs, half aware that Blake was following.

"You didn't return Chet's ring," he reminded her in a flat tone.

Raising her left hand, she glanced at the flowerlike circlet of diamonds. "No, I . . . must have forgotten." She was too tired at this point to care about such a small detàil.

When she started to lower her hand, Blake seized it and stripped the ring from her finger before she could react to stop him. He gave it a careless toss onto the polished mahogany table standing against the foyer wall.

"You can't leave valuable things lying around!" Dina instantly retrieved it, clutching it in her hand as she frowned at him—Blake, who insisted there was a place for everything and everything in its place.

"Valuable to whom?" he questioned with cool arrogance.

Her fingers tightened around the ring. "I'll keep it in my room until I can give it back to him." She waited for him to challenge her decision. When he didn't, she walked to the stairs.

"He'll be over tomorrow," Blake stated, speaking from directly behind her. "You can give it to him then."

"What time is he coming?" Dina climbed the stairs knowing she was loath to return the ring when

Blake was around, but he seemed to be leaving her little option.

"At ten for Sunday brunch."

At the head of the stairs, Dina turned. Her bedroom was the first door on the right. She walked to it only to have Blake's arm reach around her to open the door. She stopped abruptly as he pushed it open, her look bewildered.

"What are you doing?" She frowned.

"I'm going to bed." An eyebrow flickered upward as he eyed her coolly. "Where did you think I was going to sleep?"

She looked away, her gaze darting madly around. She was thrown into a trembling state of confusion by his taunting question. "I didn't think about it," she faltered. "I guess I've become used to sleeping alone."

His hand was at the small of her back, firmly directing her into the room. "Surely you don't expect that to continue?"

"I . . . ." Oh, God, yes she did. Dina realized with a frozen start. "I think it might be better . . . for a while." She stopped in the center of the room and turned to face him as he closed the door.

"You do?" Inscrutable brown eyes met her wavering look, his leathery, carved features expressionless.

"Yes, I do."

Her nerves were leaping around as erratically as jumping beans, not helped by the palpitating beat of her heart. She watched with growing apprehension as Blake peeled off his suit jacket and tie and began unbuttoning his shirt.

She tried to reason with him, her voice quivering. "Blake, it's been two and a half years."

"Tell me about it," he inserted dryly.

Her throat tightened to make her voice small. "I don't know you anymore. You're a stranger to me."

"That can be changed."

"You aren't trying to understand, Blake." Dina fought to keep control of herself. "I can't just hop into bed with—"

"Your husband?" he finished the sentence, and gave her a searing look. "Who else would you choose?"

The shirt was coming off, exposing a naked chest and shoulder tanned the same dusky shade as his face. The result heightened Dina's impression of a primitive male, powerful and dangerous, sinewy muscles rippling in the artificial light.

Her senses catapulted in alarm as she felt the force of his earthly, pagan attraction. In an attempt to break the black magic of its spell, she turned away, walking stiffly to her dresser to place Chet's ring in her jewel case.

"No one. That isn't what I meant." She remained at the dresser, her hands flattened on its top, knuckles showing white. He came up behind her and she lifted her gaze. In the dressing-table mirror her wary eyes saw his reflection join with hers. "You've become hard, Blake, a cynic," she said accusingly. "I can imagine what you've gone through...."

"Can you?" There was a faint curl of his lip. "Can you imagine how many nights I held onto my sanity by clinging to the vision of a blue-eyed woman with corn-silk hair?" His fingers twined themselves through the loose strands of her pale gold hair and Dina closed her eyes at the savage note in his voice. "Roughly nine hundred and twenty-two nights. And when I finally see her again, she's clinging to the arm of my best friend. Is it any wonder that I'm hard, bitter, when I've been waiting all this time for her lips to kiss away the gnawing memory of those hours? Did you even miss me, Dina?" With a handful of hair as leverage, he twisted her around to face him. "Did you grieve?"

Her eyes smarted with tears she refused to shed at the tugging pain in her scalp. "When you first disappeared, Blake, I was nearly beside myself with fear. But your mother was even more distraught—losing her husband, then possibly you. I had to spend most of my time comforting her. Then the company started to fall apart at the seams and Chet insisted I had to take over or it would fail. So I was plunged headfirst into another world. During the day I was too busy to think about myself, and at night there was your mother depending on me to be her strength. The only moments I had alone were in this room. And I took sleeping pills so I would get enough rest to able to get through another day. To be truthful, Blake, I didn't have time to grieve."

He was unmoved by her words, his dark eyes flat and cold. "But you had time for Chet," he accused her with icy calm.

Dina winced as the point of his arrow found its target. "It began very innocently. He was your closest friend so it was natural that he kept in touch with your mother and me. Later, there was the company connection. He was always there, bolstering me, encouraging me, and offering me a shoulder to lean on the odd moments that I needed it, without mauling me in return," she explained, refusing to sound guilty. "It grew from there after you were reported killed. I needed him."

"And I need you—now." He drew her inside the steel circle of his hands, flattening her against his chest.

The hard feel of his naked flesh beneath her hands rocked her senses. The warmth of his breath wafted over her averted face, the musky scent of him enveloping her. She pushed at his arms, straining to break out of his hold.

"You haven't listened to a word I've said!" she stormed angrily, inwardly battling against his physical arousal of her senses. "You've changed. I've changed. We need time to adjust!"

"Adjust to what?" Blake snapped. "The differences between a man and a woman? Those are differences we could discover and compensate for very quickly." The zipper of her dress was instantly undone.

"Stop it!" She struggled to keep him from sliding the dress off her shoulders. "You're making me feel like an animal!"

"You are. We both are animals, species Homosapiens." The words were issued in a cold, insensitive tone. "Put on this earth to sleep, eat and breed, to live and die. I learned in the jungle that that's the essence of our existence."

Hysterical laughter gurgled in her throat. "Oh, my God." Dina choked on the sound. "That sounds like 'You Tarzan, me Jane!'"

"Eliminate the trappings of society and the pretty words and that's what it comes down to in the end."

"No, our minds are more fully developed. We have feelings, emotions," she protested. "We...."

The dress was stripped away despite her efforts.

"Shut up!" He growled the order against her mouth and smothered the sounds when she refused to obey.

Leaning and twisting backward, Dina tried to escape the domination of his kiss, but his hands used the attempt to mold her lower body more fully to his length, her hipbones crushed by oak-solid thighs. The silk of her slip was a second skin, concealing and revealing while callused fingers moved roughly around in exploration.

Cruelly, Blake ravaged the softness of her lips. Dina thought her neck would snap under his driving force. Beneath her straining hands she felt the flexing of his muscles, smooth like hammered steel, latent in their sensuality. He was devouring her strength by degrees, slowly and steadily wearing her down. Doubling her fingers, she began hammering at him with her fists, puny blows that had little effect.

The effort seemed to use up the reserves of her strength. Within seconds, a blackness swam in front of her eyes and a dizzying weakness spread through her limbs. Her fingers dug into his shoulders and she clung to him to keep from falling into the yawning abyss that seemed to be opening in front of her.

As her resistance ebbed into nothingness, so did the brutality of his assault. The terrible bruising pressure of his mouth eased, permitting Dina to straighten her neck. Gradually she began to surface from the waves of semiconsciousness, enough to become aware of his loosened hold.

With a determined effort, she broke out of his arms. Gasping in air in panicked breaths, she backed away from him, her knees quivering. Blake swayed toward her, then stopped. A second later she realized why, as her retreat was stopped short by a wall. A cornered animal, she stared at the man who held her at bay. A stranger who was her husband.

She lifted her head, summoning all her pride to beg, "Don't do this, Blake."

Slow, silent strides carried him to her and she didn't attempt to flee. There was no mercy in his eyes and she would not submit to the ignominy of cowering. Her resistance became passive as he undressed, her eyes tightly closed.

"Are you choosing to portray the martyred wife submitting to the bestiality of her husband?" Blake taunted. "This display of frigidity is a farce. My memory wasn't damaged. I remember, too well, what a passionate lover you are."

Dina paled as she remembered, too. A flicker of the old searing fire licked through her veins as he drew her to him and her bare curves came in contact with his nude body. The tiny flame couldn't catch hold, not when the hands fanning it were callused and rough instead of the smooth, manicured hands that had once brought it to a full blaze.

"Don't destroy our marriage," she whispered, trying not to see the curling, sun-bleached hairs forming a pale cloud against the burnished bronze of his chest. "I want to love you again, Blake."

With a muffled imprecation, he buried his face in her hair. "Damn you! Why didn't you say that when I came home?" he muttered thickly in a rasping sound that suggested pain. "Why did you have to wait until now?"

"Would it have mattered?" Dina caught back a sob.

"It might have then." Effortlessly he swung her off her feet into his arms, his jaw set in a ruthless line. "I couldn't care less now. You're mine and I mean to have you."

The overhead light was switched off, throwing the room into darkness. As if guided by animal instinct, Blake carried her to the bed. Without bothering to pull down the covers, he laid her on the bed and towered beside it.

"Blake." There was an unspoken plea in the way she spoke his name, a last attempt to make him understand her unwillingness.

"No," he answered, and the mattress sagged under his weight. "Don't ask me to wait." His low voice was commanding near her ear, his breath stirring her hair. "It's been too long."

And we both have changed, Dina thought, stiffening at the moist touch of his mouth along her neck. *Can't you see the differences, Blake? Physical as well as mental. Haven't you noticed I'm wearing my hair longer?* As his hand slid over her ribs, to cup her breast, she remembered when the roundness had filled it. Now, with maturity, it overflowed.

But Blake seemed intent on discovering the ripeness of her female form, ignoring comparisons. His caressing hands roamed over her with intimate familiarity and she felt her body responding, reluctantly at first. A series of long, drugging kisses soon made her mind blank to all but the demands of her flesh.

Her senses took over, reigning supreme. She gloried in the taste of his lips probing the sensual hollows of her mouth and the brush of the soft, curling hairs on his chest hardening her nipples into erotic pebbles.

The rapidly increasing throb of her pulse was in tempo with the pagan beat of his, building to a climax. And the heady male scent of him, heightened by perspiration and his rising body heat, served to stimulate all her senses until she was filled with nothing but him.

For a time she glimpsed heights she had thought she would never see again. Blake sought all the places that brought her the most pleasure, waiting until she moaned his name in final surrender.

CHAPTER FOUR

DINA LAY IN BED, the covers pulled up to her neck, but she knew the blankets couldn't warm the chill. Her passion spent, she felt cold and empty inside as she stared upward into the darkness of the room. A tear was frozen on an eyelash.

Physically her desires had been satisfied by Blake's skilled knowledge, but she had not been lifted to the rapturous heights of a spiritual union. That only happened when there was love involved. Tonight it had been merely a mutual satisfaction of sexual desires. And that special something that had been missing eliminated the warm afterglow Dina had previously known.

Blake was beside her, their bodies not touching. An arm was flung on the pillow above his head. She could hear the steady sound of his breathing, but doubted that he was asleep. Her sideways glance sought his carved profile in the dim light. There seemed to be a grim line to his mouth, as if he was experiencing the same reaction.

As if feeling her look and hearing her question, he said in a low, flat voice, "There's one argument you didn't make, Dina. If you had, it might have prevented this disillusionment."

"What is it?" she asked in a tight, throbbing voice, longing to know what it was so she could keep this from happening again.

"The real thing can't match two and a half years of expectations."

No, she agreed silently, *not when there are no words of love exchanged, no mating of our hearts nor coming together of our souls*. It had been an act of lust, born out of anger and frustration.

"Passion never can, Blake," she murmured.

He tossed aside the blanket draped across his waist and swung his feet to the floor. Her head turned on the pillow to stare at him in the darkness.

"Where are you going?" she asked softly. Something told her that if Blake would hold her in his arms, the aching void inside her might close.

There was a faint sheen to his sun-browned skin in the shadowy light. She could make out the breadth of his shoulders and the back muscles tapering to his waist. His steps were soundless, silent animal strides.

"Another unfortunate discovery I've made since returning to civilization is that the mattresses are too soft." He spoke in a low voice, a biting, cynical tone. "I'm used to firm beds. That's what comes from spending too many nights sleeping in trees and on hard ground."

She lost him in the darkness and propped herself up on an elbow, keeping the covers tightly around her. "Where are you going?"

"To find a spare blanket and a hard floor." There was the click of the door being opened. "You have part of your wish, Dina," he added caustically. "The bed is yours. You can sleep alone."

As the door closed, a convulsive shudder ran through her. She turned her face into the pillow, curling her body into a tight ball of pain. With eyes squeezed shut, she lay there, aching for the forget-fulness of sleep.

A HAND GENTLY but persistently shook her shoulder. "Mrs. Blake? Wake up, please." Dina stirred, lashes fluttering as she tried to figure out whether or not she was imagining the voice. "Wake up, Mrs. Blake!"

But she wasn't imagining the hand on her arm. Her head throbbed dully as she opened her eyes and rolled over, dragging the covers with her. Her sleepy gaze focused on the agitated expression of the housekeeper hovering above her.

Dina became conscious of several things at once: the rumpled pillow beside her where Blake had lain so briefly, her own naked state beneath the covers, and the clothes scattered around the room—hers and Blake's. *My God, the room is a mess*, she thought.

"What is it, Deirdre?" she questioned, trying to maintain a measure of composure despite the surge of embarrassment.

The older woman bit her lip as if uncertain how to reply. "It's Mr. Blake."

The anxious look on the housekeeper's face brought an instant reaction as Dina propped herself up on her elbows, concern chasing away the remnants of sleep. "Blake? What's wrong? Has something happened to him?"

"No, it's . . . it's just that he's sleeping downstairs—on the floor in the library." A dull red was creeping up her neck into her cheeks. "And he isn't wearing any . . . any pajamas."

Dina swallowed back a smile, her relief lost in amusement. Poor Deirdre Schneider, she thought, never married in her life nor seriously close to it and probably shocked to her prim core when she found Blake sleeping in the library in the altogether.

"I see," she nodded, and tried to keep her face straight.

"Mr. Stanton will be arriving in just more than an hour." The woman was trying desperately to avoid looking at the bareness of Dina's shoulders. "I thought you should be the one to . . . to wake up Mr. Blake."

"I will," said Dina, and started to rise, then decided against adding to the housekeeper's embarrassment. "Would you hand me my robe at the foot of the bed, Deirdre?"

After handing the robe to her, the housekeeper turned discreetly away while Dina slipped into it. "Mrs. Chandler had a few things sent over yesterday for Mr. Blake," she informed Dina. "There are pajamas and a robe. I put them in the empty closet."

"I'll take them to him." Dina finished tying the sash of her robe. "And, Deirdre, tomorrow I think you'd better make arrangements with Mrs. Chandler to purchase a bed with a very firm mattress, one that's as hard as a rock."

"I will," Deirdre promised as if taking an oath. "Sorry to have awakened you, Mrs. Blake."

"That's quite all right, Deirdre," Dina answered, smiling.

With a brief self-conscious nod, the housekeeper left the room. Dina put on her slippers and walked to the small closet Deirdre had indicated. It was used mostly for storage. Amid the few boxes and garment bags hung three shirts and a brown suit. On the two inside door hooks were the pajamas and matching dressing robe in a muted shade of cranberry silk. Leaving the pajamas, Dina took the robe.

Downstairs, her hand hesitated on the knob of the library door. Tension hammered in her temples and her stomach was twisted into knots. Steeling herself to ignore the attack of nervousness, she opened the door quietly and walked in. Her gaze was directed first to the floor and its open area around the fireplace.

"Deirdre sent in the reserves, I see," Blake's male voice mocked from the side of the room.

Dina turned in its direction and saw him standing near the solid wall of shelves filled with books. A dark green blanket was wrapped around his waist, his naked torso gleaming in that deep shade of tan. Fingers had combed his thick brown hair into a semblance of order, a suggestion of unruliness remaining. Dina's pulse fluctuated in alarm, her head lifted as if scenting danger. He looked like a primitive native, proud, noble and savage.

"Did you hear her come in?" She realized it was a foolish question after she had asked it. Those long months in the jungle had to have sharpened his senses, making them more acute.

"Yes, but I decided it was wiser to pretend I was still asleep rather than shock her sensibilities," he admitted with cynical derision. "I thought she would scamper up the stairs to inform you or my mother of my lewd behavior."

Behind his veiled look Dina felt the dark intensity of his gaze scanning her face—searching for something, but she didn't know what. It made her uncomfortable and she wished she had dressed before coming down.

"I brought you a robe." She held it out to him aware of the faint trembling that wasn't yet visible.

"No doubt at Deirdre's suggestion. She must have been more shocked than I thought." But Blake made no move toward it, forcing Dina to walk to him.

"Deirdre isn't accustomed to finding naked men sleeping on the library floor," she said, defending the housekeeper's reaction and discovering a similar one in herself as Blake reached down to unwrap the blanket from around his waist. Self-consciously she averted her eyes, her color mounting as if it were a stranger undressing in front of her instead of her husband.

There was a rustle of silk, then, "It's safe to look now," Blake taunted, his mouth curving in ungentle mockery.

She flashed him an angry look for drawing attention to her sudden burst of modesty and turned away. The vein in her neck pulsed with a nervousness that she wasn't able to control. His hand touched her shoulder and she flinched from the searing contact.

"For God's sake, Dina, I'm not going to rape you!" he cursed beneath his breath. "Dammit, can't I even touch my wife?"

Her blue eyes were wide and wary as she looked over her shoulder at his fiercely burning gaze. "I don't feel like your wife, Blake," she said tightly. "I don't feel as if I'm married to you."

Immediately the fires were banked in his eyes, that freezing control that was so unlike him coming into play. "You are married to me," he stated, and walked by her to the door. Opening it, he called, "Deirdre! Bring some coffee into the library for my wife and myself." With emphasis on "wife."

"Chet is coming and I still have to dress." Dina reminded him, objecting to spending more minutes alone with him.

"He isn't due for an hour," Blake said, dismissing her protest, and walked to the leather-covered sofa, pausing beside its end table to lift the lid of the ceramic cigarette box. "Cigarette?" He flicked a questioning glance in her direction.

"No, I don't smoke. Remember?" she said with a faintly taunting arch to her voice.

"You might have acquired the habit during my absence," he shrugged.

"I didn't."

Brisk footsteps in the foyer signaled the house-keeper's approach. Seconds later she entered the library with a coffee service and two china cups on the tray she carried. A pink tint was still rouging her cheeks as Deirdre steadfastly avoided looking directly at Blake.

"Where would you like the tray?" she asked Dina.

"The table by the sofa will be fine."

Blake carried the ceramic table lighter to the cig-arette in his mouth and snapped the flame to its tip. Smoke spiraled upward and he squinted his eyes against it. Despite his show of disinterest, Dina knew he was aware of the housekeeper's every movement. After setting the tray on the table at the opposite end of the sofa from where Blake stood, Deirdre straightened up erectly.

"Will there be anything else?" Again her query was directed to Dina.

It was Blake who answered. "That will be all," he said, exhaling a thin trail of smoke. "And close the door on your way out, Deirdre."

"Yes, sir." Two red flags dotted her cheeks.

As Deirdre made a hasty exit, firmly closing the door, Blake walked to the tray. Lifting the coffee pot, he filled the two cups and offered one to Dina.

"Black, as I remember, with no sugar," he said in a tone that baited.

"Yes, thank you." Dina refused to bite as she took the cup and saucer from his hand.

Scalding steam rose from the brown liquid and Blake let his cup sit. He studied the glowing tip of his cigarette and the gossamer-thin white smoke rising upward. A wry smile crooked his mouth.

"I'd forgotten how good a cigarette can taste first thing in the morning," he mused.

Dina felt as edgy as a cat with its tail caught in a vise. She couldn't help retorting, "I thought you hadn't forgotten anything."

"Not the important things, I haven't," Blake replied, levelly meeting her irritated glance.

With a broken sigh, she wandered to the library window overlooking the expansive front lawn of the house and the cul-de-sac of its driveway. She was caught by the memory of the last time she had stared out the window in troubled silence. Oddly, it seemed an eternity ago instead of the short time that it was.

"What are you thinking about?" Blake was close, only a scant few feet behind her.

"I was merely remembering the last time I stood at this window." She sipped at the hot coffee.

"When was that?" He seemed only idly curious.

Dina felt his gaze roaming her shapely length as surely as if he touched her, and stiffened to answer bluntly, "The night of my engagement party to Chet."

"Forget about him." The command was crisp and impatient, as Dina guessed it would be.

"It isn't that easy to turn back the clock," she muttered tightly.

The cup nearly slipped from her fingers as she felt the rasping brush of his fingers against her hair. Her throat constricted, shutting off her voice and her breath.

"Have I told you I like your hair this length?" His low voice was a husky caress running down her spine.

He lifted aside the molten gold of her hair, pushing it away from her neck. The warmth of his breath against her skin warned her an instant before she glimpsed the waving darkness of his hair in her side vision.

His unerring mouth sought and found the ultra-sensitive and vulnerable spot at the base of her neck. Her heart felt as though it had been knocked sideways, and Blake took full advantage of her Achilles' heel. She felt boneless as her head tipped down and to the side to give him freer access.

The cup rattled in its saucer, but she managed to hold on to it. His arms wound around her waist to mold her back to his muscular length. For a magic second she was transported back to another time. Then a roughened hand slid under the overlapping fold of her robe to encircle the swell of her breast, a callused finger teasing its nipple, and the arms felt suddenly strange.

"Blake, no!" Weakly she tugged at his wrist, no match for his strength.

She gasped as his sensual mouth moved upward to her ear, and desire licked through her veins at the darting probe of his tongue. An all-pervading weakness went through her limbs. It was a dizzying sensation, wild drums pounding in her ears.

"Do you remember the way we used to make love in the mornings?" Blake murmured against her temple.

"Yes," she moaned, the memory all too vivid.

The cup disappeared from her hand, carried away by a fluid movement of Blake's hand. It took only the slightest pressure to turn her around. She was drawn to his side, a muscular, silk-covered thigh insinuating itself between her legs as she was arched against him. She lifted her head, subconsciously braced for the punishment of his rough kisses. Her fingers curled into his shoulders for support.

There was the tantalizing touch of his lips against hers. "After last night, I thought I had you out of my system," he said against them, "but I want you more than before."

A half sob came from her throat at the absence of

any mention of love. In the next second she didn't care, as his mouth closed over hers with sweet pressure. There was no plundering demand, only a persuasive exhorting to respond.

Her lips parted willingly, succumbing to the rapturous mastery of his exploration. The dream world of sensation seemed almost enough. She slid her fingers through the springing thickness of his hair, the scent of him earthy and clean.

As if tired of bending his head to reach her lips, Blake tightened his arm around her waist to lift her straight up, bringing her to eye level. It was another indication of his increased strength, that he should carry her weight so effortlessly. At the moment, Dina was oblivious to this example of his change.

His mouth blazed a moist trail downward to explore the pulsing vein in her neck. "Did Chet ever make you feel like this?" An attempt to exorcise the memory of Chet's kisses from her mind? Had it been motivated by nothing more than that? She pushed out of his hold, staring at him with wounded pride.

"Did he?" Blake repeated, a faintly ragged edge to his breathing.

"You'll never know," she answered in a choked voice. "Maybe he made me feel better."

He took a threatening step toward her, his features dark with rage. There was nowhere for Dina to retreat. She had to stand her ground, despite its indefensibility. Just then there was a knock at the door. Blake halted, casting an angry glance at the door.

"Who is it?" he demanded.

The door opened and Chet walked in. "I'm a bit early, but Deirdre said you were in here having coffee. She's going to bring me a cup." He stopped, as if sensing the heaviness in the atmosphere. "I didn't think you'd mind if I joined you." But it was something of a question.

"Of course not." Dina was quick to use him as a buffer.

"Come in, Chet," Blake continued the invitation. "Speak of the devil, Dina and I were just talking about you."

"Something good, I hope," Chet joked stiffly.

"Yes." Blake's dark gaze swung to Dina, a considering grimness in their depths. "Yes, it was." But he didn't explain what it had been.

She started breathing again, her hand sliding up to her throat. She became conscious of her partially clothed state and used it as an excuse to leave.

"If you two don't mind, I'll leave you to have coffee alone," she said.

"I hope you aren't going on my account," Chet said, frowning.

"No," Dina assured him quickly, avoiding Blake's mocking look. "I was going upstairs anyway to dress before Deirdre serves brunch. I'll be down shortly."

As Dina left, she met Deirdre bringing the extra cup for Chet. The housekeeper's composure was under admirable control now and she was her usual calm-faced self.

Once she was dressed, Dina slipped Chet's ring into the pocket of her dirndl skirt. At some point during the day she hoped to have the chance to return it to him while they were alone. But it was late afternoon before the opportunity presented itself.

THE PRESS HAD LEARNED of Blake's return and the house was in a state of siege for the greater part of the day. Either the doorbell or the telephone seemed to be ringing constantly. Blake had to grant interviews to obtain any peace, but his answers were concise, without elaboration, downplaying his ordeal. As his wife, Dina was forced to be at his side, while Chet adopted the role of press secretary and spokesman for the Chandler company.

Finally, at four o'clock, the siege seemed to be over and a blessed quietness began to settle over the house. Norma Chandler, who had insisted that coffee and sweets be served to all those who had come, was busy helping Deirdre clear away the mess.

The ringing of the telephone signaled a last interview for Blake, one conducted over the phone. Dina had started helping the other two women clean up. When she noticed Chet slip away to the library, she excused herself, knowing she might not have another chance to speak to him alone.

As she stepped inside the library, she saw him pouring whiskey from a crystal decanter over ice cubes in a squat glass. The engagement ring seemed to be burning a circle in her pocket.

"Would you pour me a sherry, Chet?" She quietly closed the door, shutting out Blake's voice coming from the living room.

Chet's sandy blond head lifted, his surprised look

vanishing into a smile when he say her. "Of course." He reached for another glass and a different decanter. Pouring, he remarked, "It's been quite a hectic day."

"Yes, it has." Dina walked over to take the sherry glass from his hand.

Ice clinked as Chet lifted his glass to take a quick swallow of whiskey. "A reporter that I know from one of the local papers called and got me out of bed this morning. He'd gotten wind that there was a shake-up in the Chandler hotel chain and he wanted to know what it was. I pleaded ignorance. But that's why I rushed over here so early, to warn Blake that the onslaught was coming. I knew it was only a matter of time before they found out."

"Yes." She nodded in agreement, glad there had been no announcement of their engagement in the newspaper or the reporters would have turned Blake's return into a circus.

"Blake really knows how to handle himself with the press," Chet stated with undisguised admiration.

"Yes, he does." Dina sipped at her drink.

"And it will make good publicity for the hotels," he added.

"Yes." She was beginning to feel like a puppet whose string was being pulled to nod agreement to everything Chet said—when it really wasn't what she wanted to talk about at all.

"I imagine somebody in the company let it slip about Blake." He stared thoughtfully at the amber liquid in his glass. "I called around to all the major officers yesterday to let them know he was back. That's probably how the word got out."

"Probably," Dina agreed, and promptly took the initiative to lead into her own subject. "Chet, I've been wanting to see you today, alone—" she reached in her pocket to take out the circlet of diamonds "—to return this to you."

He took it from her outstretched hand, looking boyishly uncomfortable. His thumb rubbed it between his fingers as he stared at it, not meeting the sapphire brightness of her gaze.

"I don't want you to get the idea that I was deserting you yesterday." His voice was uncertain, almost apologetic. "But I know how you felt about Blake and I didn't want to stand in the way of your happiness."

With the explanation given for the way he had so readily abandoned their engagement, Chet lifted his head to gaze at her earnestly, a troubled shade of clouded blue in his eyes. Affection rushed through Dina at his unselfishness, sacrificing his wants for hers.

"I understand, Chet."

Relief glimmered in his smile. "You must really be glad to have him back."

"I . . . ." She started to repeat the positive assertion she had been making all day, ready to recite the words automatically, but she stopped herself. Among other things, Chet was her best friend, as well as Blake's. With him she could speak her mind. "He's changed, Chet."

He hesitated for a second before answering, as if her response had caught him off guard and he wanted to word his reply carefully.

"Considering all Blake has been through, it's bound to have left a mark on him," he offered.

"I know, but . . . ." She sighed, agitated and frustrated because she couldn't find the words to explain exactly what she meant.

"Hey, come on now," Chet cajoled, setting his glass down and grasping her gently by the shoulders, his head bent down to peer into her apprehensive face. "When two people care as much about each other as you and Blake do, they're bound to work out their differences. It just can't happen overnight," he reasoned. "Now come on. What do you say? Let's have a little smile. You know it's true that nothing is ever as bad as it seems."

Mountains and molehills. Reluctantly almost, her lips curved at his coaxing words. His steadying influence was having its effect on her again.

"That's my girl!" he grinned.

"Oh, Chet," Dina declared with a laughing sigh, and wrapped her arms lightly around him, taking care not to spill her drink. She hugged him fondly. "What would I do without you?" She drew her head back to gaze at him.

"I hope neither of us has to find out," he remarked, and affectionately kissed the top of her nose.

The knob turned and the library door was pushed open by Blake. At the sight of Dina in Chet's arms he froze, and the same paralysis gripped her. She paled as she saw his lips thin into an angry line.

But the violence of his emotion wasn't detectable in his voice as he remarked casually, "Is this a private party or can anyone join?"

His question broke the chains holding Dina

motionless. She withdrew her arms from around Chet to hold her sherry glass in both hands. Chet turned to greet him, insensitive to the heightening tension in the air.

"Now that you're here, Blake, we can drink a toast to the last of the newspaper reporters," he announced in a celebrating tone, not displaying any self-consciousness about the scene Blake had interrupted.

"For a while anyway," Blake agreed, his gaze swinging to Dina. "What are you drinking?"

"Sherry." There would be no explosion now, Dina realized. Blake would wait until they were alone.

"I'll have the same."

It was late that evening before Chet left. Each dragging minute in the interim honed Dina's nerves to a razor-thin edge. By the time he had left, she could no longer stand the suspense of waiting for the confrontation with Blake.

With the revving of Chet's car coming from the driveway, Dina paused in the foyer to challenge Blake. "Aren't you going to say it?"

He didn't pretend an ignorance of her question, his gaze hard and unrelenting. "Stay away from Chet."

All the blame for the innocent encounter was placed on her, and she reacted with indignant outrage. "And what about Chet?"

"I know Chet well enough to be assured he isn't going to trespass, unless encouraged, on my territory."

"So I'm supposed to avoid him, is that it?" she flashed.

"Whatever relationship you had with him in my absence is finished," Blake declared in a frigid tone. "From now on he's simply an acquaintance of mine. That's all he is to you."

"That's impossible!" She derided his suggestion that she could dismiss Chet from her life with a snap of her fingers. "I can't forget all he's meant to me that easily."

A pair of iron clamps dug into the soft flesh of her arms and she was jerked to him, the breath knocked out of her by the hard contact with the solid wall of his chest. Her lips were crushed by the angry fire of his kiss, a kiss that seared his brand of possession on her and burned away any memory of another's mouth.

Dina was released from his punishing embrace with equal force. Shaken and unnerved, she retreated a step. With the back of her hand she tried to rub away the fiery imprint of his mouth.

"You—" she began with impotent rage.

"Don't push me, Dina!" Blake warned.

They glared at each other in thundering silence. Dina had no idea how long the battle of wills would have continued if his mother hadn't entered the foyer seconds later. Each donned a mask to conceal their personal conflict from her eyes.

"Deidre just told me you'd asked her to bring some blankets to the library, Blake." Norma Chandler was wearing a frown. "You aren't going to sleep there again tonight, are you?"

"Yes, I am, mother," he responded decisively.

"But it's so uncivilized," she protested.

"Perhaps," Blake conceded, for an instant meeting Dina's look. "It's also infinitely preferable to not sleeping."

"I suppose so." His mother sighed her reluctant agreement. "Good night, dear."

"Good night, mother," he returned, and coldly arched an eyebrow at Dina. "Good night."

CHAPTER FIVE

THE LIBRARY DOOR stood open when Dina came down the stairs the next morning. She smoothed a nervous hand over her cream linen skirt and walked to the dining room where breakfast coffee and juice were already on the table. But there was no sign of Blake. Dina helped herself to juice and coffee and sat down.

"Isn't Blake having breakfast this morning?" she questioned the housekeeper when she appeared.

"No, ma'am," Deirdre replied. "He's already left. He said he was meeting Jake Stone for breakfast and going to the office from there. Didn't he tell you?"

"Yes, I believe he did," Dina lied, and forced a smile. "I must have forgotten."

"Mrs. Chandler was most upset about it," the woman remarked with a knowing nod.

Dina frowned. "Because Blake is meeting the attorney?"

"No, because he's going into the office. Mrs. Chandler thought he should wait a few days. I mean, he just came back and all, and right away he's going to work," Deirdre explained.

"He's probably anxious to see how everything is." There was a smug feeling of satisfaction that he would find the entire operation running smoothly knowing that a great deal of the credit was hers.

"What will you have this morning, Mrs. Blake? Shall I fix you an omelet?"

"I think I'll just have juice and coffee, Deirdre, thank you." She wanted to be at the office when Blake arrived to be able to see his face when he realized how capably she had managed in his absence.

"As you wish," the housekeeper sniffed in disapproval.

The morning traffic seemed heavier than usual and Dina chafed at the delay it caused. Still she arrived at the office building well within her usual time. As she stepped out of the elevator onto the floor the company occupied, she was relieved that Chet had already notified the various executive personnel of Blake's return and that she was spared that task. She would have time to go over her notes on the departmental meeting this afternoon and have much of the Monday morning routine handled before Blake arrived.

She breezed down the corridor to her office, keeping her pace brisk while she nodded greetings and returned good mornings to the various employees along the way. She didn't want to stop and chat with anyone and use up her precious time. She felt very buoyant as she entered the office of her private secretary.

"Good morning, Amy," she said cheerfully.

"Good morning, Mrs. Chandler." The young woman beamed back a smile. "You're in good spirits this morning."

"Yes, I am," Dina agreed. Her secretary was going through the morning mail and she walked to her desk to see if there was anything of importance she should know about before Blake arrived.

"Your good spirits wouldn't have anything to do with Mr. Chandler's coming back, would they?" Amy Wentworth inquired with a knowing twinkle. Dina wasn't obliged to make a comment as her secretary continued, "All of us here are so happy he's back safely."

"So am I, Amy," Dina nodded, and glanced over the girl's shoulder for a glimpse at the mail. "Anything special in the mail this morning?"

"Not so far," her secretary replied, returning her attention to the stack of letters.

"Any calls?"

"Only one. Mr. Van Patten called."

"Did he leave a message?" Dina asked, her quick perusal of the mail completed.

"Oh, no," Amy hastened to explain. "Mr. Chandler took the call."

"Mr. Chandler?" she repeated. "Do you mean Blake is already here?"

"Yes, he's in the office." Amy motioned towards Dina's private office. "I'm sure he won't mind if you go right on in, Mrs. Chandler."

For several seconds Dina was too stunned to speak. It was *her* office, her pride protested. And *her* secretary was grandly giving her permission to enter it. Blake had moved in and managed to convey the impression that she had moved out.

Her blue eyes darkened with rage. Turning on her heel, she walked to the private office. She didn't bother to knock, simply pushing the door open and walking in. Blake was seated behind the massive walnut dest—*her* desk! He glanced up when she entered. The arrogantly inquiring lift of his eyebrow lit the fuse of her temper.

"What are you doing here?" she demanded.

"I was about to ask you the same question," countered Blake with infuriating calm.

"It happens to be *my* office and that's *my* secretary outside!" Dina retorted. Her flashing eyes saw the papers in his hands and she recognized the notes as those she had been going to go over for the departmental meeting that afternoon. "And those are *my* notes!"

He leaned back in the swivel chair, viewing her tirade with little emotion. "I was under the impression that all of this—" he waved his hand in an encompassing gesture "—belonged to the company."

"I happen to be in charge of the company," she reminded him.

"You *were* in charge of the company," Blake corrected her. "I'm taking over now."

She was trembling violently now, her anger almost uncontrollable. She fought to keep her voice low and not reveal how thoroughly he had aroused her.

"You're taking over," she repeated. "Just like that!" She snapped her fingers.

"Your job is done." Blake shrugged and fingered the papers on the desk. "And excellently, from all that I've seen this morning."

It was the compliment she had sought, but not delivered the way she had intended it to be. Therefore it brought no satisfaction; the thunder was stolen from her glory.

"And what am I supposed to do?" she demanded.

"Go home. Go back to being my wife." His sun-
roughened features wore a frown, as if not understanding why she was so upset.

"And do what?" challenged Dina. "Twiddle my
thumbs all day until you come home? Deirdre does
all the cooking and the cleaning. It's your mother's
house, Blake. There's nothing for me to do there."

"Then start looking for an apartment for us. Or
better yet, a house of our own," he suggested.
"That's what you wanted before, a place of our own
that you could decorate the way you wanted it."

A part of her wanted it still, but it wasn't the
motivating force in her life. "That was before,
Blake," she argued. "I've changed. If we did have a
house and the decorating was all done the way I
wanted it, what would I do then? Sit around and
admire my handiwork? No, I enjoy my work here.
It's demanding and fulfilling."

He was sitting in the chair, watching her with
narrowed eyes. "What you're saying is you enjoy
the power that goes along with it."

"I enjoy the power," Dina admitted without hesitation, a hint of defiance in the tightness of her
voice. "I enjoy the challenge and the responsibility,
too. Men don't have a monopoly on those feelings."

"What are you suggesting, Dina? That we reverse
our roles and I become the house husband? That I
find the house, do all the decorating, cleaning and
entertaining?"

"No, I'm not suggesting that." Confusion was
tearing at her. She didn't know what the solution
was.

"Perhaps you'd like me to take another flight to South America and this time not bother to come back?"

"No, I wouldn't—and stop twisting my words!"

Hot tears flooded her eyes, all the emotional turmoil inside her becoming too much to control. She turned sharply away, blinking frantically at the tears, trying to force them back before Blake saw them.

There was a warning squeak of the swivel chair as Blake rose and approached her. Her lungs were bursting, but she was afraid to take a breath for fear it would sound like a sob.

"Is this the way you handle a business disagreement?" he lashed out in impatient accusation.

Aware that he towered beside her, Dina kept her face averted so he wouldn't see the watery blue of her eyes. "I don't know what you mean," she lied.

His thumb and fingers clamped on her chin and twisted it around so he could see her face. "Do you usually indulge in a female display of tears when you don't get your own way?"

The wall of tears was so solid that Dina could barely see his face. "No," she retorted pushing at the hand that held her chin. "Do you always attack on a personal level whenever someone doesn't agree with you wholeheartedly?"

She heard his long impatient sigh, then his fingers curved to the back of her neck, forcing her head against his chest. An arm encircled her to draw her close. His embrace was strong and warm, but Dina made herself remain indifferent to Blake's attempt to comfort her. She felt the pressure of his chin resting atop her head.

"Would you mind telling me what the hell I'm supposed to do about this?" Blake muttered.

She wiped at the tears with shaking fingers and sniffed, "I don't know."

"Here." He reached inside his suit jacket to hand her his handkerchief. There was a light rap on the door and Blake stiffened. "Who is it?" he snapped, but the door was already opening.

Self-consciously Dina tried to twist out of his arms, but they tightened around her as if closing ranks to protect her. She submitted to their hold, her back to the door.

"Sorry," she heard Chet apologize with a trace of chagrin. "I guess I've gotten used to walking in unannounced."

He must have made a move to leave because Blake said, "It's all right. Come on in, Chet." Unhurriedly he withdrew his arms from around Dina. "You'll have to excuse Dina. She still gets emotional once in a while about my return," he said to explain away her tears and the handkerchief she was using to busily wipe away their traces.

"That's understandable," said Chet, "I came in to let you know everyone's here. They're waiting in the meeting room."

His statement lifted Dina's head with a start. "Meeting?" She picked up on the word and frowned. "There isn't any meeting scheduled on my agenda this morning."

"I called it," Blake announced smoothly, his bland gaze meeting her sharp look. Then he shifted his attention to Chet in a dismissing fashion. "Tell them I'll be there in a few minutes."

"I will." And Chet left.

At the click of the closing door, Dina turned roundly on Blake, her anger returning. "You weren't going to tell me about the meeting, were you?" she accused him.

Blake walked to the desk and began shuffling through the papers on top of it. "Initially, no. I didn't see the need to tell you."

"You didn't see the need?" Dina sputtered at his arrogantly dismissive statement.

"To be truthful, Dina—" he turned to look at her, his bluntly chiseled features seeming to be carved out of teakwood "—it didn't occur to me that you would come into the office today."

"Why ever not?" She stared at him in confusion and disbelief.

"I assumed you would be glad, if not grateful, to relinquish charge of the company to me. I thought you saw yourself as a stopgap president and would relish being free of the burdens of responsibility. I thought you would be happy to resume the role of a homemaker."

"You obviously don't know me very well," Dina retorted.

"So I'm beginning to discover," Blake responded grimly.

"What now?" she challenged him.

"No man likes to compete with his wife for a job, and I have no intention of doing so with you," he stated.

"Why not?" Dina argued. "If I'm equally competent—"

"But you are not," Blake interrupted, his eyes turning into dark chips of ironstone.

"I am." Surely she had proven that.

He ignored the assertion. "In the first place, our age difference alone gives me fourteen more years of experience in the business than you. Secondly, my father put me to work as a busboy when I was fifteen. Later I was a porter, a desk clerk, a cook, a manager. Compared to mine, your qualifications are negligible."

His logic deflated her balloon of pride. He made her seem like a fool, a child protesting because a toy was taken away. Dina had learned how to disguise her feelings and she used the skill to her advantage.

"You're probably quite right," she said stiffly. "I'd forgotten how much of a figurehead I was. Chet did the actual running of the company."

"Don't be ridiculous!" Blake dismissed the statement with a contemptuous jeer. "Chet is incapable of making an important decision."

Her eyes widened at the accusation. "How can you say that? He's been so loyal to you all these years, your best friend."

The lashing flick of his gaze laughed at her reference to Chet's loyalty, reminding her of Chet's engagement to her, but he made no mention of it when he spoke. "Just because he's been my friend doesn't mean I'm blind to his faults."

Although puzzled, Dina didn't pursue the topic. It was dangerous ground, likely to turn the conversation to a more personal level. At the moment, she wanted to keep it on business.

"None of that really matters. It still all comes down to the same basic thing—I'm out and you're in."

Blake raked a hand through his hair, rumpling it

into attractive disorder. "What am I supposed to do, Dina?" he demanded impatiently.

"That's up to you," she shrugged, feigning cold indifference while every part of her rebelled at the emptiness entering her life. "If you don't object to my borrowing *your* secretary, a letter formally tendering my resignation will be on *your* desk when you return from your meeting."

"No, I don't object." But Blake bristled at her cutting sarcasm. As she turned on her heel to leave, he covered the distance between them with long strides, grabbing at her elbow to spin her around. "What do you expect me to do?" His eyes were a blaze of anger.

"I don't know—"

He cut across her words. "Do you want me to offer you a position in the administration? Is that it?"

Excited hope leaped into her expression. After Blake had put it into words, she realized that that was exactly what she wanted—to still have a part in running the company, to be involved in its operation.

"Dammit, I can't do it, Dina!" Blake snapped.

Crushed, she demanded in a thin voice, "Why?"

"I can't go around sweeping people out of office so you can take their place. Disregarding the fact that it smacks of nepotism, it implies that I don't approve of the people you hired to fill key positions. The logical deduction from that would be that I believed you'd done an inadequate job of running the company in my absence." His expression was hard and grim. "It's going to be several years before

I can make any changes without them reflecting badly on you."

"That settles it, then, doesn't it?" Her chin quivered, belying the challenge in her voice.

His teeth were gritted, a muscle leaping along his jaw. "If you weren't my wife..." he began, about to offer another explanation of why his hands were tied in this matter.

"That's easily remedied, Blake," Dina flashed, and pulled her arm free before his grip could tighten. She didn't expect it to last long, but he made no attempt to recapture her.

"That's where you're wrong." He clipped out the words with biting precision.

Inwardly quaking under his piercing look, Dina turned away rather than admit his power to intimidate her. "It's immaterial anyway," she said with a small degree of composure. "My resignation will be on your desk within an hour." She walked to the door.

"Dina." The stern command of his voice stopped her from leaving.

She didn't remove her hand from the doorknob or turn to face him. "What?"

"Maybe I can keep you on in an advisory capacity." The stiffness of his words took away from the conciliatory gesture.

"I don't want any favors! And certainly not from the great Blake Chandler!" Dina flared, and yanked open the door.

It closed on a savage rush of expletives. When Dina turned away from the door, she looked into the curious and widened gaze of the secretary, Amy

Wentworth. Dina silently acknowledged that the walls of the private office were thick, but she doubted if they were thick enough to deafen the sound of voices raised in argument. She wondered how much of the aftereffect of her quarrel with Blake was apparent in her face. She strained to appear composed and in command of herself as she walked to Amy's desk.

"Put aside whatever you're doing, Amy," she ordered, trying to ignore the widening look she received.

"But . . . ." The young secretary glanced hesitantly toward the inner office Dina had just left, as if uncertain whether she was to obey Dina or Blake.

Dina didn't give her a chance to put her thoughts into words. "I want you to type a letter of resignation—for me. You know the standard form of these things. Just keep it simple and direct. Effective immediately."

"Yes, Mrs. Chandler," Amy murmured, and immediately removed the dustcover from her electric typewriter.

The connecting office door was pulled open and Dina glanced over her shoulder to see Blake stride through. She could tell he had himself under rigid control, but it was like seeing a predatory animal restrained in chains. The minute the shackles were removed, he would pounce on his prey and tear it apart. And she was his prey.

Yet, even knowing she was being stalked, she was mesmerized by the dangerous look in his gaze. She waited motionless as he walked toward her, the force of his dark vitality vibrating over her nerve ends, making them tingle in sharp awareness.

"Dina, I . . . ." Blake never got the rest of his sentence out.

Chet entered the room through the door to the outer corridor. "Oh, I see you're on your way," he concluded at the sight of Blake. "I was just coming to see how much longer you'd be." His gaze switched its attention to Dina and became a troubled blue as he noticed the white lines of stress on her face.

"Yes, I'm on my way," Blake agreed crisply, and looked back at Dina. "I want you to attend the meeting, Dina." The veiled harshness in his gaze dared her to defy him.

But Dina felt safe in the company of others. "No. It's better for everyone to realize that you're in charge now and not confuse them by having a former head of the company present." She saw his mouth thin at her response and turned away in a gesture of dismissal.

"Dina has a good point," Chet offered in agreement, but a darting look from Blake made him vacillate. "Of course, unless you think it's wiser to—"

"Let's go," Blake snapped.

In a silent storm, he swept from the room, drawing Chet into his wake and leaving Dina feeling drained and colorless. Her nerves seemed to be delicate filaments, capable of snapping at the slightest pressure. When the letter of resignation was typed, her hand trembled as she affixed her signature to it.

"Put it on Mr. Chandler's desk," she ordered, and returned it to Amy.

"It was nice working for you, Mrs. Chandler,"

the young secretary offered as Dina turned to go,
the words spoken in all sincerity.

"Thank you, Amy." Dina smiled mistily, then
hurried from the room.

Leaving the building, she walked to her car. She
knew there was no way she could return to the
house and listen to Mother Chandler's happy conversation about Blake's return. With the top down
on the white sports car, she removed the scarf from
her hair and tucked it in the glove compartment.

With no destination in mind, she climbed into the
car and drove, the wind whipping at her hair, which
glittered like liquid sunlight in the morning air.
Around and through the back streets, the main
streets, the side streets of the city of Newport she
went.

Half the time she was too blinded by tears to
know where she was. She didn't notice the row of
palatial mansions on Bellevue Avenue, or the
crowds gathered on the wharf for the trial of the
America Cup races.

She didn't know who she was, what she was, or
why she was. Since Blake's return, she was no
longer Dina Chandler. She was once again Mrs.
Blake Chandler, lost in her husband's identity. She
was no longer a businesswoman, nor did she feel
like a housewife, since she had no home and a
stranger for a husband. As to the reason why, she
was in total confusion.

It was sheer luck that she glanced at the dash-
board and noticed the gasoline gauge was hovering
at the empty mark. Practicality forced her out of the
bewildering whirlpool of questions. They stayed

away until she was parked in a gas station and waiting in the building where her tank was being filled.

Then they returned with pounding force and Dina reeled under the power of them. Her restlessly searching gaze accidentally spied the telephone inside the building. She walked blindly to the phone and, from long habit, dialed the number of the one person who had already seen her through so much emotional turmoil.

The impersonal voice of an operator answered and Dina requested in an unsteady voice, "Chet Stanton, please."

"Who is calling, please?"

Dina hesitated a fraction of a second before answering, "A friend."

There was a moment when Dina thought the operator was going to demand a more specific answer than that, then she heard the call being put through. "Chet Stanton speaking," his familiar voice came on the line.

"Chet, this is Dina," she rushed.

"Oh." He sounded surprised and guarded. "Hello."

She guessed at the cause for the way he responded. "Are you alone?"

"No."

Which meant that Blake must be in his office. Dina wasn't certain how she knew it was Blake and not someone else, but she was positive of it.

"Chet, I have to talk to you. I have to see you," she declared in a burst of despair. Glancing at her wristwatch, she didn't give him a chance to reply. "Can you meet me for lunch?"

She heard the deep breath he took before he answered, "I'm sorry, I'm afraid I've already made plans for lunch."

"I have to see you," she repeated. "What about later?"

"It's been a long time since I've seen you." Chet began to enter into the spirit of the thing, however uncertainly. "Why don't we get together for a drink? Say, around five-thirty?"

It was so long to wait, she thought desperately, but realized it was the best he could offer. "Very well," she agreed, and named the first cocktail lounge that came to mind.

"I'll meet you there," Chet promised.

"And, Chet—" Dina hesitated "—please don't say anything to Blake about meeting me. I don't want him to know. He wouldn't understand."

There was a long pause before he finally said, "No, I won't. See you then."

After hanging up the receiver, Dina turned and saw the gas station attendant eyeing her curiously, yet with a measure of concern. She opened the pocketbook slung over her shoulder and started to pay for the gasoline.

"Are you all right, miss?" he questioned.

She glimpsed her faded reflection in the large plate-glass window of the station and understood his reason for asking. Her hair was windblown, and in riotous disorder. Tears had streaked the mascara from her lashes to make smutty lines around her eyes. She looked like a lost and wayward urchin despite the expensive clothes she wore.

"I'm fine," she lied.

In the car, she took a tissue from her bag and wiped the dark smudges from beneath her eyes. A brush put her tangled mass of silky gold hair into a semblance of order before it was covered by the scarf she had discarded.

"You have to get hold of yourself," she scolded her reflection in the rearview mirror.

Turning the key in the ignition, she started the powerful motor of the little car and drove away, wondering what she was going to do with herself for the rest of the day.

CHAPTER SIX

TYPICALLY, THE LOUNGE was dimly lit. Overhead lighting was practically nonexistent and the miniature mock lanterns with their small candle flames flickering inside the glass chimneys provided little more. The dark wood paneling of the walls offered no relief, nor did the heavily beamed low ceiling.

Tucked away in an obscure corner of the lounge, Dina had a total view of the room and the entrance door. A drink was in front of her, untouched, the ice melting. Five more minutes, her watch indicated, but it already seemed an interminable wait.

An hour earlier she had phoned Mother Chandler to tell her she would be late without explaining why or where she was. Blake would be angry, she realized. *Let him*, was her inward response. The consequences of her meeting with Chet she would think about later.

Brilliant sunlight flashed into the room as the door was opened. Dina glanced up, holding her breath and hoping that this time it might be Chet. But a glimpse of the tall figure that entered the lounge paralyzed her lungs. Her heart stopped beating, then skyrocketed in alarm.

Just inside the lounge, Blake paused, letting his eyes adjust to the gloom. There was nowhere Dina could run without drawing his attention. She tried

to make herself small, hoping he wouldn't see her in
this dim corner of the room. Dina felt rather than
saw his gaze fasten on her seconds before his pur-
poseful strides carried him to her table.

When he stopped beside her, Dina couldn't look
up. Her teeth were so tightly clenched they hurt.
She curled her hands around the drink she hadn't
touched since it had been set before her. Despite
the simmering resentment she felt, there was a sense
of inevitability, too. Blake didn't speak, waiting for
Dina to acknowledge him first.

"Imagine meeting you here," she offered in a bitter tone of mock surprise, not letting her gaze lift
from the glass cupped in her hands. "Small world,
isn't it?"

"It's quite a coincidence," he agreed.

There was a bright glitter in her blue eyes when
she finally looked at him. His craggy features were
in the shadows, making his expression impossible to
see. The disturbing male vitality of his presence
began to make itself felt despite her attempt to
ignore it.

"How did you know I was here?" she demanded,
knowing there was only one answer he could give.

And Blake gave it. "Chet told me."

"Why?" The broken word came out unknowingly, directed at the absent friend who had betrayed
her trust.

"Because I asked him."

"He promised he wouldn't tell you!" Her voice
was choked, overcome by the discovery that she
was lost and completely alone in her confusion.

"So I gathered," Blake offered dryly.

Dina averted her gaze to breathe shakily. "Why did he have to tell you?"

"I am your husband, Dina, despite the way you try to forget it. That gives me the right to at least know where you are."

His voice was as smooth as polished steel, outwardly calm and firm. Her gaze noticed his large hands clenched into fists at his side, revealing the control he was exercising over his anger. He was filled with a white rage that his wife should arrange to meet another man. Dina was frightened, but it was fear that prompted the bravado to challenge him.

"You were in Chet's office when I called, weren't you?" she said accusingly.

"Yes, and I could tell by the guilty look on his face that he was talking to you. After that, it didn't take much to find out what was going on."

"Who did you think I would turn to? I needed him." Dina changed it to present tense. "I need Chet."

Like the sudden uncoiling of a spring, Blake leaned down, spreading his hands across the tabletop, arms rigid. In the flickering candlelight his features resembled a carved teakwood mask of some pagan god, harsh and ruthless and dangerously compelling.

"When are you going to get it through that blind little brain of yours that you've never needed him?" he demanded.

Her heart was pounding out a message of fear. "I don't know you," she breathed in panic. "You're a stranger. You frighten me, Blake."

"That makes two of us, because I'm scared as hell of myself!" He straightened abruptly, issuing an impatient, "Let's get out of here before I do something I'll regret."

Throwing caution away, Dina protested, "I don't want to go anywhere with you."

"I'm aware of that!" His hand clamped a hold on her arm to haul her to her feet, overpowering her weak resistance. Once she was upright, his fingers remained clamped around her arm to keep her pressed to his side. "Is the drink paid for?" Blake reminded her of the untouched contents of the glass on the table.

As always when she came in physical contact with him, she seemed to lose the ability to think coherently. His muscular body was like living steel and the softness of her shape had to yield. Everything was suddenly reduced to an elemental level. Not until Blake had put the question to her a second time did Dina take in what he had asked.

She managed a trembling, "No, it isn't."

Releasing her, Blake took a money clip from his pocket and peeled off a bill, tossing it on the table. Then the steel band of his arm circled her waist to guide her out of the lounge, oblivious to the curious stares.

In towering silence he walked her to the white Porsche, its top still down. He opened the door and pushed her behind the wheel. Then, slamming the door shut, he leaned on the frame, an unrelenting grimness to his mouth.

"My car is going to be glued to your bumper, following you every inch of the way. So don't take any detours on the route home, Dina," he warned.

Before Dina could make any kind of retort, he walked to his car parked in the next row of the lot. Starting the car, she gunned the motor as if she were accelerating for a race, a puny gesture of impotent defiance.

True to his word, his car was a large shadow behind hers every block of the way, an ominous presence she couldn't shake even if she had tried—which she didn't. Stopping in the driveway of his mother's house—their house—Dina hurried from her car, anxious to get inside where the other inhabitants could offer her a degree of safety from him.

Halfway to the door Blake caught up with her, a hand firmly clasping her elbow to slow her down.

"This little episode isn't over yet," he stated in an undertone. "We'll talk about it later."

Dina swallowed the impulse to challenge him. It was better to keep silent with safety so near. Together they entered the house, both concealing the state of war between them.

Mother Chandler appeared in the living-room doorway, wearing an attractive black chiffon dress. Her elegantly coiffed silver hair was freshly styled, thanks to an afternoon's appointment at her favorite salon. She smiled brightly at the pair of them, unaware of the tension crackling between them.

"You're both home—how wonderful!" she exclaimed, assuming her cultured tone. "I was about to suggest to Deirdre that perhaps she should delay dinner for an hour. I'm so glad it won't be necessary. I know how much you detest overcooked meat, Blake."

"You always did like your beef very rare, didn't

you, Blake?" Dina followed up on the comment, her gaze glittering at his face with diamond sharpness. "I have always considered your desire for raw flesh as a barbaric tendency."

"It seems you were right, doesn't it?" he countered.

Mother Chandler seemed impervious to the barbed exchange as she waved them imperiously into the living room. "Come along. Let's have a sherry and you can tell me about your first day back at the office, Blake." She rattled on, covering their tight-lipped silence.

IT WAS AN ORDEAL getting through dinner and making the necessary small talk to hide the fact that there was anything wrong. It was even worse after dinner when the three of them sat around with their coffee in the living room. Each tick of the clock was like the swing of a pendulum, bringing nearer the moment when Blake's threatened discussion would take place.

The telephone rang and the housekeeper answered it in the other room. She appeared in the living room seconds later to announce, "It's for you, Mr. Blake. A Mr. Carl Landstrom."

"I'll take it in the library, Deirdre," he responded.

Dina waited several seconds after the library door had closed before turning to Mother Chandler. "It's a business call." Carl Landstrom was head of the accounting department and Dina knew that his innate courtesy would not allow him to call after office hours unless it was something important. "Blake is probably going to be on the phone for a while," she explained, a fact she was going to use to make her escape and avoid his private talk. "Would you explain to him that I'm very tired and have gone on to bed?"

"Of course, dear." The older woman smiled, then sighed with rich contentment. "It's good to have him back, isn't it?"

It was a rhetorical question, and Dina didn't offer a reply as she bent to kiss the relatively smooth cheek of her mother-in-law. "Good night, Mother Chandler."

"Good night."

Upstairs, Dina undressed and took a quick shower. Toweling herself dry, she wrapped the terry-cloth robe around her and removed the shower cap from her head, shaking her hair loose. She wanted to be in bed with the lights off before Blake was off the telephone. With luck he wouldn't bother to disturb her. She knew she was merely postponing the discussion, but for the moment that was enough.

Her nightgown was lying neatly at the foot of the bed as she entered the bedroom that adjoined the private bath, her hairbrush in hand. A few brisk strokes to unsnarl the damp curls at the ends of her hair was all that she needed to do for the night, she decided, and sat on the edge of the bed to do it.

The mattress didn't give beneath her weight. It seemed as solid as the seat of a wooden chair. Dina was motionless as she assembled the knowledge and realized that the new mattress and box springs she had ordered for Blake had arrived and hers had been removed.

She sprang from the bed as if discovering a bed

of hot coals beneath it. No, her heart cried, she couldn't sleep with him—not after that last humiliating experience; not with his anger simmering so close to the surface because of today.

The door opened and Blake walked in, and the one thing in the forefront of her mind burst out in panic. "I'm not going to sleep with you!" she cried.

A brow flicked upward. "At the moment, sleep is the furthest thing from my mind."

"Why are you here?" She was too numbed to think beyond the previous moment.

"To finish our discussion." Blake walked to the chair against the wall and motioned toward the matching one. "Sit down."

"No," Dina refused, too agitated to stay in one place even though he sat down with seemingly relaxed composure while she paced restlessly.

"I want to know why you were meeting Chet." His hooded gaze watched her intently, like an animal watching its trapped prey expend its nervous energy before moving in for the kill.

"It was perfectly innocent," she began in self-defense, then abruptly changed her tactics. "It's really none of your business."

"If it was as perfectly innocent as you claim," Blake said, deliberately using her words, "then there's no reason not to tell me."

"What you can't seem to understand, or refuse to understand, is that I need Chet," she flashed. "I need his comfort and understanding, his gentleness. I certainly don't receive that from you!"

"If you'd open your eyes once, you'd see you're not receiving it from him, either," Blake retorted.

"Don't I?" Her sarcastic response was riddled with disbelief.

"Chet doesn't comfort. He merely mouths the words you want to hear. He's incapable of original thought."

"I would hate to have you for a friend, Blake," she declared tightly, "if this is the way you regard friends when they aren't around, cutting them into little pieces."

"I've known Chet a great deal longer than you have. He can't survive unless he's basking in the reflected glory of someone else. When I disappeared, he transferred his allegiance to you, because you represented strength. He's a parasite, Dina, for all his charm," Blake continued his cold dissection. "He lived on your strength. He persuaded you to take charge of the company because he knew he was incapable of leading a child, let alone a major corporation."

"You don't know what you're saying," Dina breathed, walking away from his harsh explanation.

"The next time you're with him, take a good look at him, Dina," he ordered. "And I hope you have the perception to see that you've been supporting him through all this, not the other way around."

"No!" She shook her head in vigorous denial.

"I should have stayed away for a couple more months. Maybe by then the rose-colored spectacles would have come off and you would have found out how heavily he leans on you."

Pausing in her restless pacing, Dina pressed her hands over her ears to shut out his hateful words. "How can you say those things about Chet and still call him your friend?"

"I know his flaws. He's my friend in spite of them," Blake responded evenly. "Yet you were going to marry him without acknowledging that he had any."

"Yes. Yes, I was going to marry him!" Dina cried, pulling her hands away from her ears and turning to confront him.

"Only when I came back, he dropped you so fast it made your head swim. Admit it." Blake sat unmoving in the chair.

"He wanted me to be happy," she argued defensively.

"No," he denied. "My return meant you were on the way out of power and I was in. Chet was securing his position. There was nothing chivalrous in his reason for breaking the engagement. He wasn't sacrificing anything, only insuring it."

"So why did you hound him into admitting he was meeting me today?" challenged Dina.

"I didn't hound him. He was almost relieved to tell me."

"You have an answer for everything, don't you?" She refused to admit that anything Blake was saying made any sense. She fought to keep that feeling of antagonism; without it, she was defenseless against him. "It's been like this ever since you came back," she complained, uttering her thoughts aloud.

"I knew when everyone discovered I was alive, it was going to be a shock. But I thought it would be a pleasant shock," Blake sighed with wry humor. "In your case, I was wrong. It was a plain shock and you haven't recovered from it yet."

Dina heard the underlying bitterness in his tone

and felt guilty. She tried to explain. "How did you think I would feel? I'd become my own person. Suddenly you were back and trying to absorb me again in your personality, swallow me up whole."

"How did you think I would react when you've challenged me every minute since I've returned?" His retaliation was instant, his temper ignited by her defensive anger, but he immediately brought it under control. "It seems we've stumbled onto the heart of our problem. Let's see if we can't have a civilized discussion and work it out."

"Civilized!" Dina laughed bitterly. "You don't know the meaning of the word. You spent too much time in the jungle. You aren't even civilized about the way you make love!"

Black fires blazed in his eyes. The muscles along his jaw went white from his effort to keep control. "And you go for the jugular vein every time!" he snarled, rising from the chair in one fluid move.

Dina's heart leaped into her throat. She had aroused a beast she couldn't control. She took a step backward, then turned and darted for the door. But Blake intercepted her, spinning her around, his arms circling her, crushing her to his length.

His touch sizzled through her like an electric shock, immobilizing her. She offered not an ounce of resistance as his mouth covered hers in a long, punishing kiss. She seemed without life or breath, except what he gave her in anger.

Anger needs fuel to keep it burning, and Dina gave him none. Gradually the brutal pressure eased and his head lifted a fraction of an inch. She opened her eyes and gazed breathlessly into the brilliant darkness of his. The warm moistness of his breath was caressing her parted lips.

His hand stroked the spun gold of her hair, brushing it away from her cheek. "Why do you always bring out the worst in me?" he questioned huskily.

"Because I won't let you dominate me the way you do everyone else," Dina whispered. She could feel the involuntary trembling of his muscular body and the beginnings of the same passionate tremors in her own.

"Does it give you a feeling of power—" he kissed her cheek " to know that " his mouth teased the curling tips of her lashes "—you can make me lose control?" He returned to tantalize the curving outline of her lips. "You are the only one who could ever make me forget reason."

"Am I?" Dina breathed skeptically, because he seemed in complete control at the moment and she was the one losing her grip.

"I had a lot of time to think while I was trying to fight my way out of that tropical hell. I kept remembering all our violent quarrels that got started over the damnedest things. I kept telling myself that if I ever made it back, they were going to be a thing of the past. Yet within hours after I saw you, we were at each other's throats."

"I know," she nodded.

As if believing her movement was an attempt to escape his lips, Blake captured her chin to hold her head still. With languorous slowness, his mouth took possession of hers. The kiss was like a slow-burning flame that kept growing hotter and hotter.

Its heat melted Dina against his length, so hard and very male. Her throbbing pulse sounded loudly in her ears as the flames coursed through her body.

Before she succumbed completely to the weakness of her physical desire, she twisted away from his mouth. She knew what he wanted, and what she wanted, but she had to deny it.

"It won't work, Blake." Her throat worked convulsively, hating the words even as she said them. "Not after the last time."

"The last time . . . . " He pursued her lips, his mouth hovering a feather's width from them, and she trembled weakly, lacking the strength to turn away. "I hated you for becoming engaged to Chet, even believing I was dead. And I hated myself for not having the control to stop when you asked me not to make love to you. This time it's different."

"It's no good." But the hands that had slipped inside her robe and were caressing her skin with such arousing thoroughness felt very good.

For an instant Dina didn't think Blake was going to pay any attention to her protest, and she wasn't sure that she wanted him to take note of it. Then she felt the tensing of his muscles as he slowly became motionless.

He continued to hold her in his arms as if considering whether to concede to her wishes or to overpower her resistance, something he could easily accomplish in her present half-willing state.

A split second later he was setting her away from him, as if removing himself from temptation. "If that's what you want, I'll wait," he conceded grimly.

"I . . . ." In a way, it wasn't what she wanted; and Dina almost said so, but checked herself. "I need time."

"You've got it," Blake agreed, his control superb, an impenetrable mask concealing his emotions. "Only don't make me wait too long before you come to a decision."

"I won't." Dina wasn't even certain what decision there was to make. What were her choices?

His raking look made her aware of the terry robe hanging loosely open, exposing the cleavage of her breasts. She drew the folds together to conceal the naked form Blake knew so well. He turned away, running his fingers through the wayward thickness of his dark hair.

"Go to bed, Dina," he said with a hint of weariness. "I have some calls to make."

Her gaze swung to the bed and the quilted spread that concealed the rock-hard mattress. "The new box spring and mattress that I had Deirdre order for you came today, and she put it in here. I'll . . . I'll sleep in the guest room."

"No." Blake slashed her a look over his shoulder. "You will sleep with me, if you do nothing else."

Dina didn't make the obvious protest regarding the intimacy of such an arrangement and its frustrations, but offered instead, "That bed is like lying on granite."

There was a wryly mocking twist of his mouth. "To use an old cliché, Dina, you've made your bed, now you have to lie in it."

"I won't," she declared with a stubborn tilt of her chin.

"Am I asking too much to want my wife to sleep beside me?" He gave Dina a long, level look that she couldn't hold.

Averting her head, she closed her eyes to murmur softly "No, it isn't too much."

The next sound she heard was the opening of the door. She turned as Blake left the room. She stared at the closed door that shut her inside, wondering if she hadn't made a mistake by giving in to his request.

Walking over to the bed, she pressed a hand on the quilt to test its firmness. Under her full weight it gave barely an inch. It was going to be quite a difference from the soft mattress she usually slept on, but then her bed partner was a completely different man from the urbane man she had married. Dina wondered which she would get used to first—the hard bed or the hard man?

Nightgowned, with the robe lying at the foot of the bed, she crawled beneath the covers. The unyielding mattress wouldn't mold to her shape, so she had to attempt to adjust her curves to it, without much success. Sleep naturally became elusive as she kept shifting positions on the hard surface trying to find one that was comfortable.

Almost two hours later she was still awake, but she closed her eyes to feign sleep when she heard Blake open the door. It was difficult to regulate her breathing as she listened to his quiet preparations. Keeping to the far side of the bed, she stayed motionless when he climbed in to lie beside her, not touching but close enough for her to feel his body heat.

Blake shifted a few times, then settled into one position. Within a few minutes she heard him breathing deeply in sleep. Sighing, she guessed she was still hours away from it.

CHAPTER SEVEN

A HAND WAS MAKING rubbing strokes along her upper arm, pleasantly soothing caresses. Then fingers tightened to shake her gently.

"Come on, Dina, wake up!" a voice ordered.

"Mmm." The negative sound vibrated from her throat as she snuggled deeper into her pillow.

Only it wasn't a pillow. There was a steady thud beneath her head, and the pillow that wasn't a pillow moved up and down in a regular rhythm. No, it wasn't a pillow. She was nestled in the crook of Blake's arm, her head resting on his chest. She could feel the curling sun-bleached hairs on his chest tickling her cheek and nose.

Sometime in the night she had forsaken the hardness of the mattress to cuddle up to the warm hardness of his body. Her eyelids snapped open at the familiarity sleep had induced. Dina would have moved away from him, but the arm around her tightened to hold her there for another few seconds.

A callused finger tipped her chin upward, forcing her to look at him, and her heart skipped a beat at the lazy warmth in the craggy male face.

"I'd forgotten what it was like to sleep with an octopus," Blake murmured. "Arms and legs all over the place!"

Heat assailed Dina at the intimacy of her position. Sleep had dulled her reflexes. When his thumb touched her lips to trace their outline, Dina was too slow in trying to elude it. As the first teasing brush made itself felt, she lost the desire to escape it. Rough skin lightly explored every contour of her mouth before his thumb probed her lips apart to find the white barrier of her teeth.

It became very difficult to breathe under the erotically stimulating caress, especially when his gaze was absorbing every detail of his action with disturbing interest. Situated as she was, with a hand resting on the hard muscles of his chest, afraid to move, Dina felt and heard the quickening beat of his pulse. Hers was racing no less slowly.

The muffled groan of arousal that came from his throat sent the blood rocketing through her heart. The arm around her ribcage tightened to draw her up. His mouth renewed the exploration his thumb had only begun. With a mastery that left her shattered, Blake parted her lips, his tongue seeking out hers to ignite the fires of passion.

In the crush of his embrace, it was impossible for Dina to ignore the fact that Blake was naked beneath the covers. It was just as impossible to be unaware that her nightgown was twisted up around her hips. It was a discovery his roughly caressing hands soon made.

As his hands slid beneath it, his fingers catching the material to lift it higher, Dina made a weak attempt to stop him. It seemed the minute her own hands came in contact with the living bronze of his muscled arms, they forgot their intention.

More of her bare skin came in contact with his

hard flesh. The delicious havoc it created with her senses only made Dina want to feel more of him. Willingly she slipped her arms from the armholes as Blake lifted it over her head. His mouth was absent from her lips for only that second. The instant the nightgown was tossed aside, he was back kissing her with a demanding passion that she eagerly returned.

Blake shifted, rolling Dina onto her back, the punishing hardness of the mattress beneath her. His sun-bronzed torso was above her, an elbow on the mattress offering him support. His warm, male smell filled her senses, drugging her mind. When he dragged his mouth away from hers, she curved a hand around his neck to bring it back. Blake resisted effortlessly, the burning darkness of his gaze glittering with satisfaction at her aroused state.

At sometime the covers had been kicked aside. As his hand began a slow, intimate exploration of her breasts, waist and hips, Blake watched it, his eyes drinking in the shapely perfection of her female form. The blatant sensuality of the look unnerved Dina to the point that she couldn't permit it to continue. Again came the feeling that it was a stranger's eyes looking at her, not those of her husband.

Gasping back a sob, she tried to roll away from him and reached the protective cover of the sheets and blankets. Blake thwarted the attempt, forcing her back, his weight crushing her to the unyielding mattress that had already bruised her muscles and bones.

"No, Dina, I want to look at you," Blake insisted in a voice husky with desire. "I imagined you like this so many times, lying naked in the bed beside me, your body soft and eager to have me make love to you. Don't blame me for wanting to savor this moment. This time no screech of a jungle bird is going to chase away this image. You are mine, Dina, mine."

The last word was uttered with possessive emphasis as his head descended to stake its first claim, his mouth seeking her lips, kissing them until passion overrode her brief attempt at resistance. A languorous desire consumed her as he extended his lovemaking to more than just her lips. She quivered with fervent longing at the slow descent of his mouth to her breasts, favoring each of them in turn to the erotic stimulations of his tongue.

Under his sensuous skill, Dina forgot the strangeness of his arms and the hardness of the rocklike mattress beneath her. She forgot all but the dizzying climb to the heights of gratification and the dazzling view from the peak. They descended slowly, not finding their breath until they reached the lower altitudes of reality.

Dina lay enclosed in his arms, her head resting on his chest as it had when she had awakened. This time there was a film of perspiration coating his hard muscles and dampening the thick, wiry hairs beneath her head. Dina closed her eyes, aware that she had come very close to discovering her love for Blake again, its light glittered in the far recesses of her heart.

Blake's mouth moved against her hair. "I had forgotten what an almost insatiably passionate little wench you are." His murmured comment suddenly brought the experience down to a purely physical level. What had bordered on an act of love, became lust. "I enjoyed it. Correction, I enjoyed you," he added, which partially brought the light back to her heart.

Crimsoning, Dina rolled out of his arms, an action he didn't attempt to prevent. The movement immediately caused a wince of pain. Every bone and fiber in her body was an aching reminder of the night she had spent in the hard-rock bed.

"How can you stand to sleep in this bed?" Dina was anxious to change the subject, unwilling to speak of the passion they had just shared. "It's awful."

"You'll get used to it." When Blake spoke, Dina realized he had slid out of bed with barely a sound while she had been discovering her aches and pains. Her gaze swung to him as he stepped into the bottoms of his silk pajamas and pulled them on. Feeling her eyes watching him, Blake glanced around. There was a laughing glint in his dark eyes as he said, "It's a concession to Deirdre and her Victorian modesty this morning."

Dina smiled. Even that hurt. "What time is it?"

"Seven," he answered somewhat absently, and rubbed the stubble of beard on his chin.

"That late?"

Her pains deserted her for an instant and she started to rise, intent only on the thought that she would be late getting to the office unless she hurried. Then she remembered she no longer had any reason to go to the office and sank back to the mattress, tiredness and irritation sweeping over her.

"Why am I getting up?" she questioned herself aloud. "It took me so long to get to sleep last night. Why didn't you just let me keep right on sleeping?" Then he wouldn't have made love to her and she wouldn't be experiencing all this confusion and uncertainty, about herself and him.

"You'd be late to work," was Blake's even response.

"Have you forgotten?" Bitterness coated her tongue. "I've been replaced. I'm a lady of leisure now."

"Are you?" He gave her a bland look. "Your boss doesn't think so."

"What boss? You?" Dina breathed out with a scornful laugh. "You're only my husband."

"Does that mean you're turning it down?"

"What? Will you quit talking in riddles?"

"Maybe if you hadn't been so proud and stubborn yesterday morning and attended the meeting as I asked you to, you'd know what I'm talking about."

She pressed a hand against her forehead, tension and sleeplessness pounding between her eyes. "I didn't attend the meeting, so perhaps you could explain."

"We're starting a whole new advertising campaign to upgrade the image of the Chandler Hotel chain," he explained. "We can't possibly compete with the bigger chains on a nationwide basis, especially when most of our hotels are located in resort areas, not necessarily heavily populated ones. We're going to use that fact to our advantage. From now on, when people think of resort hotels, it's going to be synonymous with Chandler Hotels."

"It's a sound idea," Dina conceded. "But what does that have to do with me?"

"You're going to be in charge of the campaign."

"What?" Blake's calm announcement brought her upright, wary disbelief and skepticism in the look she gave him. "Is this some kind of a cruel joke?"

There was an arrogant arch to one dark eyebrow. "Hardly." He walked around the bed to where she stood. "I put the proposal to the rest of the staff yesterday, along with the recommendation that you handle it."

"Is this a token gesture? Something for me to do to keep me quiet?" She couldn't accept that there wasn't an ulterior motive behind the offer. It might mean admitting something else.

"I admit that picking you as my choice to head the campaign was influenced by the tantrum you threw in the office yesterday morning when you discovered I was taking over." His gaze was steady, not yielding an inch in guilt. "But you can be sure, Dina, that I wouldn't have suggested your name to the others if I didn't believe you could handle the job. You can put whatever interpretation you like on that."

Dina believed him. His candor was too forthright to be doubted, especially when he acknowledged the argument they had had earlier. It surprised her that he had relented to this extent, putting her in charge of something that could ultimately be so important to the company. True, she would be working for him, but she would be making decisions on her own, too.

"Why didn't you tell me about this last night?" She frowned. "Your decision had already been made. You just said a moment ago that you told the staff yesterday. Why did you wait until now to tell me?"

Blake studied her thoughtfully. "I was going to tell you last night after we'd had our talk, but circumstances altered my decision and I decided to wait."

"What circumstances?" Dina persisted, not following his reasoning.

"To be perfectly honest, I thought if you knew about it last night you might have been prompted to make love to me out of gratitude," Blake replied without a flicker of emotion appearing in his impassive expression.

There was an explosion of red before her eyes. "You thought I'd be so grateful that I'd...." Anger robbed her of speech.

"It was a possibility."

Dina was so blind with indignant rage that she couldn't see straight, but it didn't affect her aim as her opened palm connected with the hard contour of his cheek. As the white mark turned scarlet, Blake walked into the bathroom. Trembling with the violence of her aroused temper, Dina watched him go.

When her anger dissipated, she was left with a niggling question. If he hadn't made that degrading remark, would she still be angry with him? Or would this have been the first step towards reestablishing the foundation of their marriage, with Blake recognizing that she had the talent and skill to be more than a simple housewife? Hindsight could not provide the answer.

At the breakfast table, their conversation was frigidly civil.

"Please pass the juice."

"May I have the marmalade?"

That fragile mood of shy affection they had woken up to that morning was gone, broken by the doubting of each other's motives.

When both had finished breakfast, Blake set his cup down. "You may ride to the office with me this morning," he announced.

"I would prefer to take my own car."

"It's impractical for both of us to drive."

"If you had to work late, I would be without a way home," Dina protested.

"*If* that should arise, you may have the car and *I'll* take a taxi home," he stated, his demeanor cold and arrogant.

Dina was infuriatingly aware that Blake would have an argument for every excuse she could offer. "Very well, I'll ride with you." She gave in with ill grace.

The morning crush of Newport traffic seemed heavier than normal, the distance to the office greater, the time passing slower, and the polar atmosphere between them colder than ever.

Feeling like a puppy dog on a leash, Dina followed Blake from the parking lot to his office. There she sat down, adopting a business air to listen to specific suggestions that had been offered by Blake and the staff for the campaign. It was a far-reaching plan, extending to redecorating some hotels to meet with their new resort image.

At that one, Dina couldn't help commenting caustically, "I'm suprised I'm not limited to that task. Decorating is woman's work, isn't it?"

The thrust of his frigid gaze pierced her like a cold knife. "Do you want to discuss this program intelligently? Or do you want to bring our personal difficulties into it? Because if you do, I'll find someone else for the job."

Her pride wanted to tell him to find that person, but common sense insisted she would ultimately be the loser if she did. The project promised to be a challenge, and Dina had come to enjoy that. Her pride was a bitter thing to swallow, but she managed to get it down.

"Sorry. That remark just slipped out." She shrugged. "Go on."

There was a second's pause as Blake weighed her words before continuing. When he had concluded, he gave her a copy of the notes from the staff meeting and a tentative budget.

Dina glanced over them, then asked, "Where am I to work?"

"I'll take you to your new office."

She followed him out of the office and walked beside him down the long corridor until they came to the end. Blake opened the last door.

"Here it is."

The metal desk, chair and shelves seemed to fill up the room. Three offices this size could have fit into Blake's office, Dina realized. And that wasn't all. It was cut off from the other staff offices, at the end of the hall, isolated. She could die in there and nobody would know, she thought to herself.

Blake saw the fire smoldering in her blue eyes. "This is the only office that was available on such short notice," he explained.

"Is it?" she retorted grimly.

"Yes—" he clipped out the word challengingly "—unless you think I should have moved one of the executive staff out of his or her office to make room for you."

Dina knew that would have been illogical and chaotic, with records being shifted and their exact location possibly unknown for several days. Still, she resented the size and location of her new office, regardless of how much she accepted the practicality of its choice. But she didn't complain. She didn't have to, since Blake knew how she felt.

She looked at the bare desk top and said, "There's no telephone?"

"Arrangements have already been made to have one installed today."

"Fine." She walked briskly into the room, aware of Blake still standing in the doorway.

"If you have any questions—" he began in a cool tone.

Dina interrupted, "I doubt if I will." The banked fires of her anger glittered in the clear blue of her eyes.

His gaze narrowed, his expression hardening. "You can be replaced, Dina."

"Permanently?" she drawled in a taunting kitten-purr voice.

For an instant she thought he might do away with her violently, but instead he exhibited that iron control and pivoted to walk away. There was a tearing in her heart as he left. Dina wondered if she was deliberately antagonizing him or merely reacting to his attempted domination of her.

Pushing the unanswerable question aside, she set to work, taking an inventory of the supplies on hand and calculating what she would need. After obtaining the required items from the supply room, she began making a list of information she would need before drawing up a plan of action for the advertising campaign.

At the sound of footsteps approaching the end of the hallway, she glanced up from her growing list. She had left the door to her office open to lessen the claustrophobic sensation, and she watched the doorway, curious as to who would be coming and for what reason.

Chet appeared, pausing in the doorway, a twinkle in his gray blue eyes, an arm behind his back. "Hello there," he smiled.

"Are you lost or slumming?" Dina questioned with a wry curve to her lips.

He chuckled and admitted, "I was beginning to think I was going to have to stop and ask directions before I found you."

"It's certain I'm not going to be bothered with people stopping by to chat on their way someplace else. This is the end of the line," she declared with a rueful glance around the tiny office. "Which brings me to the next obvious question."

"What am I doing here?" Chet asked it for her. "When I heard you were exiled to the far reaches of the office building, I decided you might like a cup of hot coffee." The arm that had been behind his

back moved to the front to reveal the two Styrofoam cups of coffee he was juggling in one hand.
"At least, I hope it's hot. After that long walk, it
might be cold."

"Hot or lukewarm, it sounds terrific." Dina
straightened away from the desk to relax against the
rigid back of her chair. "I shall love you forever for
thinking of it."

She had tossed out the remark without considering what she was saying, but she was reminded of it
as a discomfited look flashed across Chet's face.

"I guess that brings me to the second reason why
I'm here." He lowered his head as he walked into
the room, not quite able to meet her gaze.

"You mean about not meeting me yesterday and
sending Blake in your place," Dina guessed, accu-
rately as it turned out.

"Yes, well—" Chet set the two cups on the desk
top "—I'm sorry about that. I know you didn't
want me to tell Blake and I wouldn't have, either,
except that he was in my office when you called and
he guessed who I was talking to."

"So he said," she murmured, not really wanting
to talk about it in view of the discussion she had
with Blake last night regarding Chet.

"Blake didn't lay down the law and forbid me to
go or anything like that, Dina."

"He didn't?" she breathed skeptically.

"No. He asked if you sounded upset," Chet
explained. "When I said that you did, he admitted
that the two of you were having a few differences
and he thought it was best that I didn't become
involved in it. He didn't want me to be put in the

position of having to take sides when both of you
are my friends."

Friends? Dina thought. Just a few days ago, Chet
had been her fiancé, not her friend. But he looked
so pathetically sorry for having let her down yesterday that she simply couldn't heap more guilt on his
bowed head.

Instead she gave him the easy way out. "Blake
was right, it isn't fair to put you in the middle of our
disagreements. If I hadn't been so upset I would
have realized it. Anyway, it doesn't matter now."
She shrugged. "It all worked out for the best." That
was a white lie, since it almost had, until their
blowup that morning.

"I knew it would." The smile he gave her was
tinged with relief. "Although I wasn't surprised to
hear Blake admit that the two of you had got off to
a rocky start." He removed the plastic lid from the
cup and handed the cup to her.

"Why do you say that?" she asked.

"The two of you were always testing each other
to see which was the stronger. It looks like you still
are."

"Which one us is the stronger? In your opinion,"
Dina qualified her question.

"Oh, I don't know." His laughter was accompanied by a dubious shake of his head. "A feeling of
loyalty to my own sex makes me want to say Blake,
but I have a hunch I would be underestimating
you."

In other words, Dina realized, Chet was not taking sides. He was going to wait until there was a
clear-cut winner. In the meantime he was keeping
his options open, buttering up both of them.

The minute the last thought occurred to her, Dina knew it had been influenced by Blake's comment that Chet was always beside the one in power. But she immediately squashed the thought as small and not deserving of someone as loyal as Chet.

"You're a born diplomat, Chet." She lifted the coffee cup in a toast. "No wonder you're such an asset to this company."

"I try to be," he admitted modestly, and touched the side of his cup to hers. "Here's to the new campaign."

The coffee was only medium hot and Dina took a big sip of it. Chet's reference to the new project made her glance at the papers, notes and lists spread over her desk.

"It's going to be quite a formidable project." She took a deep breath, aware of the magnitude of the image change for the Chandler Hotel chain. "But I can feel it's right and that it will be very successful."

"That's the third reason I'm here."

Her startled gaze flew to his face, her blue eyes rounded and bright with inquiry. "Why?"

Had she made Blake so angry that he was already taking her off the campaign? Oh, why hadn't she held her tongue, she thought, angered by the way she had kept pushing him

"Blake wants me to work with you on it," Chet announced.

Her relief that Blake hadn't replaced her didn't last long. "Doesn't he think I'm capable of handling it by myself?" Her temper flared at the implied doubt of her ability.

"You wouldn't be here if he didn't believe you

could," he said placatingly. "But after all, you said it yourself. It's going to be a formidable project and you're going to need some help. I've been nominated to be your help. Besides, Blake knows how well we worked together as a team while he was gone."

Dina counted to ten, forcing herself to see the logic of Chet's explanation. But she wasn't sure that she liked the idea. There was still the possibility that Blake had appointed Chet as her watchdog and he would go running to Blake the instant she made a mistake.

She was doing it again, she realized with a desperate kind of anger. She was not only questioning Blake's motives, but making accusations against Chet's character, as well. Damn Blake, she thought, for putting doubts about Chet in her mind.

Chet took a long swig of his coffee, then set it aside. "Where shall we begin?"

"I've been making some lists," Dina readjusted her attention to the project at hand.

She went over the lists with Chet, discussing various points with him. Although Dina was still skeptical of Blake's motives in having Chet assist her, she accepted it at face value until she could prove otherwise. An hour later, Chet left her small office with a formidable list of his own to carry out.

The bulk of the day Dina spent getting the project organized. In itself, that was no easy task. At five o'clock, she was going over the master list again, making notes in the margins while various ideas were still fresh in her mind.

"Are you ready?" Blake's voice snapped from the open doorway.

Her head jerked up at the sound. The lenses of her glasses blurred his image, deceptively softening the toughness of his features. For an instant, Dina almost smiled a welcome, then the sharpness of his demanding question echoed in her mind. Recovering from that momentary rush of pleasure, Dina bent her head over the papers once again.

"I will only be a few more minutes." She adjusted the glasses on the bridge of her nose.

Blake walked in, his dislike at being kept waiting charging the air with tension. He sat in the straight-backed chair in front of her desk. Dina was conscious of his scrutiny, both of her and her work.

"Since when did you wear glasses?" he accused.

She touched a finger to a bow, realizing he had never seen her wearing them. "I began wearing them about a year ago."

"Do you need them?"

"What a ridiculous question!" she snapped. "Of course, I need them."

"It isn't so ridiculous," Blake contradicted with dry sarcasm. "They enhance the image of a crisp, professional career woman who has turned her back on domestic pursuits."

It was a deliberately baiting comment. Dina chose not to rise to the tempting lure. "With all the reading and close work I have had to do, it became too much of a strain on my eyes. After too many headaches, I put my vanity aside and began wearing glasses to read. They have nothing to do with my image," she lied, since the choice of frame styles had been made with that in mind.

"Then you do admit to having an image," he taunted her coldly.

It was no use. She simply couldn't concentrate on what she was doing. It took all of her attention to engage in this battle of words with him. Removing her glasses, she slipped them into their leather case. Dina set her notes aside and cleared the top of her desk.

"You haven't answered my question," Blake prompted in a dangerously quiet voice when she rose to get her coat.

"I hadn't realized your comment was a question." She took her purse from the lower desk drawer, unconsciously letting it slam shut to vent some of her tightly controlled anger.

"Is that how you see yourself, Dina, as a career woman whose life is centered around her work, with no time for a husband?" This time Blake phrased it as a question. The office was so small that when he stood up, he was blocking her path.

"That is hardly true." She faced him, her nerves quivering with his closeness.

"No?" An eyebrow lifted in challenging disbelief.

"Have you forgotten?" It was bravado that mocked him. "I was going to marry Chet, so I must have felt there was room for a husband in my life."

"I am your husband," Blake stated.

"I don't know you." Dina looked anywhere but into those inscrutable dark eyes.

"You knew me well enough this morning, in the most intimate sense of the word that a wife can 'know' her husband," Blake reminded her deliberately.

"This morning was a mistake." She brushed past him to escape into the hallway, but he caught her arm to half turn her around.

"Why was it a mistake?" he demanded.

"Because I let myself listen to all your talk about long, lonely nights and I started feeling sorry for you, that's why," Dina lied angrily, because she was still confused by her willingness to let him make love to her this morning when he still remained so much of a stranger to her in many ways.

His mouth thinned into a cruel line, all savage and proud. "Compassion is the last thing I want from you!" he snarled.

"Then stop asking me to pick up the threads of our life. The pattern has changed. I don't know you. The Blake Chandler that spent two and a half years in a jungle is a stranger to me. You may have had to live like an animal, but don't ask me to become your mate. I am more than just an object to satisfy your lust." The words streamed out, flooding over each other in their rush to escape. With each one, his features grew harder and harder until there was nothing gentle or warm left in them.

Blake gave her a push towards the door. "Let's go before you goad me into proving that you're right," he snapped.

Aware that she had nearly wakened a sleeping tiger whose appetites were ravenous, Dina quietly obeyed him. All during the ride back to his mother's house she kept silent, not doing anything to draw attention to herself. Blake ignored her, not a single glance straying to her. The cold war had briefly exploded into a heated battle, but once again the atmosphere was frigid.

Within minutes of entering the house, Blake disappeared into the library. Dina found herself alone in the living room with her mother-in-law, listening to the latest gossip Norma Chandler had picked up at the afternoon's meeting of the garden club.

"Of course, everyone was buzzing with the news about Blake," the woman concluded with a beaming smile. "They wanted to know every single detail of his adventure in the jungle. I thought they were never going to let me leave. Finally I had to insist that I come home to be here when you and Blake arrived."

Dina was certain that Norma Chandler had been the center of attention. No doubt, the woman had reveled in it, even if the spotlight had been a reflection of her son's.

"It was a thoughtful gesture to be waiting at the door when Blake came home from the office," she murmured, knowing some appreciation should be expressed. It was expected.

"I only wish he had waited a few more days before returning to the office," sighed Norma Chandler. "After all he's been through, he was entitled to rest for a few days."

Unspoken was the fact that it would have given her a chance to dote on him, coddle him like a little boy again. But the chance had been denied her and Norma Chandler was protesting. Dina wasn't sure if she was being blamed for Blake's decision to return to work so quickly. In case she was, she decided to set the record straight.

"It wasn't my idea that he had to come back right away. Blake has some bold, new plans for the company. I think he was eager to get back to work so he could put them into operation," Dina explained.

"I am sure you are right, but he isn't giving us much time to enjoy the fact that he is back. There I go," Norma Chandler scolded herself. "I'm complaining when I should be counting my blessings. It's just that I can't help wondering how much longer I'll have him."

"That's a peculiar thing to say," Dina frowned.

"You will probably be moving out soon—into a place of your own, won't you? Then I'll only be able to see him on weekends," she pointed out.

"We have discussed the possibility of getting a place of our own," Dina admitted, choosing her words carefully as she recalled their argument the previous morning. "But I don't think it will happen in the near future. We both will probably be too busy to do much looking. Naturally we don't want to move into just any place," she lied.

It wasn't that Dina had become so career-oriented that she didn't long for a home of her own as she had led Blake to believe. At the moment, she was relieved to live in the Chandler home where his mother and the housekeeper could serve as buffers. She wasn't ready yet to share a home solely with the stranger who was her husband. Maybe she never would be.

"I won't pretend that I'm not glad to hear you say that." Her mother-in-law smiled broadly at the statement. "You know how much I have enjoyed having you live here, Dina. Now that Blake is back, my happiness has been doubled. There is something about having a man around the house that makes it seem more like a home."

"Yes," Dina agreed, if not wholeheartedly.

"I don't like to pry." There was a hesitancy in the woman's voice and expression. "But I have the feeling that there is a bit of tension between you and Blake. If I am wrong, you just say so or tell me to mind my own business. I don't want to become an interfering mother-in-law, but—" Her voice trailed off in the expectancy of a response from Dina.

It was Dina's turn to hesitate. She doubted if Mother Chandler would understand, but she felt a need to confide her fears in someone.

"There is a tension between us," she admitted cautiously. "It's just that Blake has changed. And I have changed. We aren't the same people we were two and a half years ago."

"It's Chet, isn't it?" Norma Chandler drew her own conclusions, hardly listening to what Dina had said. "I know that Blake behaved in front of the others as if he understood and forgave, but it bothered him, didn't it?"

"To a certain extent, yes." But not to the degree that her mother-in-law was implying.

"It is only natural that he'd be upset to find his wife engaged to his best friend, but he'll come around. In a few years, you'll be laughing about it."

"Probably," Dina nodded, but she couldn't help wondering if they would be together in a few years. For that matter, she wondered if they would be together in a few months.

The housekeeper entered the living room. "Dinner is ready whenever you wish," she announced.

"Now is fine, Deirdre," Norma Chandler stated. "Blake is in the library. Would you please tell him?"

Dinner that evening was an awkward meal, one

that was made more awkward because Norma
Chandler seemed determined to convince Blake
how very properly Dina had behaved during his
absence. Dina knew it was an outgrowth of their
conversation and there was simply no way she
could intervene. Blake seemed indifferent to the
praise his mother heaped on Dina, which only
prompted Norma Chandler to pile more on.

It was a relief to escape to the privacy of the bedroom after coffee had been served. The tension of
the day and the evening had tightened her muscles
into taut bands. The sight of the bed and the
thought of sleeping beside Blake another night
increased the tension. She was the captive of a crazy
confusion, torn between dreading the idea of Blake
making love to her again and looking forward to
the possibility.

Dina walked from the bedroom into the private
bath that adjoined it. She filled the porcelain tub
with hot water and added a liberal amount of
scented bubble bath. From her bedroom closet, she
brought her robe and hung it on a door hook. Shed-
ding her clothes, Dina stepped into the tub and submerged herself up to her neck in the steamy mound
of bubbles.

Lying back in the tub, she let the warm water
soak away the tension, and slowly relaxed in the
soothing bath. The lavender fragrance of the bubbles wafted through the air, a balm to her senses.
The water cooled and Dina added more hot, losing
track of time in her watery cocoon.

The bedroom door opened and closed. Dina
heard it, but she wasn't unduly concerned that

Blake had come to the room. The bathroom door was closed. She expected him to respect the desire for privacy it implied.

When the bathroom door was opened anyway, Dina sat up straight in a burst of indignation. The sound of sloshing water drew Blake's gaze. Minus his suit jacket and tie, he had unbuttoned the front of his shirt down to his stomach, exposing a disturbing amount of hard muscled flesh and dark chest hairs.

"Sorry, I didn't know you were in here," he apologized insincerely.

The bubbles had been slowly dissipating during her long soak. Only a few bits of foam remained around the uplifting curve of her breasts. The fact did not escape Blake's attention. It kept him from leaving.

Self-consciously Dina grabbed for a handcloth, holding it in front of her. "Now that you've discovered I'm in here, get out."

"I thought you might want me to wash your back, or wouldn't you consider that civilized behavior?" Blake mocked.

"I don't need my back washed, thank you." Dina wasn't sure why she had bothered with the washcloth. It was becoming wet and very clingy. "Please leave," she requested stiffly. "I'm finished with my bath and I'd like to get out of the tub."

"I'm not stopping you. The sooner you are out, the sooner I can take my shower." Blake turned and walked into the bedroom, closing the door behind him.

Not trusting him, Dina quickly rinsed away the

bubbles that were drying on her skin and stepped out of the tub. After rubbing herself down with the towel, she slipped into her robe and zipped it to the throat. Another few minutes were spent tidying the bathroom.

When she entered the bedroom, her senses were heightened to a fever pitch. Blake was sitting on the love seat, smoking a cigarette, his posture seemingly indolent. His hooded gaze swept over her.

"It's all yours." Dina waived a hand toward the bathroom.

Blake stubbed out his cigarette and uncoiled his length from the love seat. "Thank you." His response was cool and tauntingly lacking in gratitude.

Dina suppressed a shudder at his freezing politeness and wondered whether their heated exchanges were preferable to this. As he crossed the room, she walked to the closet. At the door, she stopped to glance at him.

It suddenly became imperative that she make him understand that she was not going to let him persuade her to make love, not until she was able to sort out her true feelings for him. She wanted to end this sensation that she was married to a stranger before they shared any further intimacies.

"Blake, I have no intention—" Dina began.

"Neither have I," he cut in sharply and paused at the doorway to the bathroom to pin her with his gaze. His mouth slanted in a cruel line. "I won't be exercising my husbandly rights with you. Didn't you think I was capable of phrasing it politely?" Blake mocked the sudden paleness of her complex ion. "Perhaps if I had promised not to rape you, it would have been more in keeping with your image of me, wouldn't it?"

Dina turned away from his caustic challenge. "As long as we understand each other," she murmured stiffly.

"Just so there isn't any mistake. I won't touch you again until you come to me. And you will come to me, Dina." There was something almost threatening in the savagely controlled tone he used.

The closing of the bathroom door left Dina shaken. She changed out of her robe into her nightgown without being aware of her actions. She heard the shower running in the bathroom and tried not to visualize Blake standing beneath its spray, all sun-browned flesh, naked and hard, as paganly virile as a jungle god.

Shaking away the heady image, she walked to the bed and folded down the satin coverlet. Dina was between the silk sheets when Blake came out of the bathroom, a towel wrapped around his waist. He didn't glance her way as he switched off the light and walked around to the opposite side of the bed, unerringly finding his way in the dark. The mattress didn't give beneath his weight, but she was aware of him. The sheets seemed to transmit the heat from his nude body.

A tidal way of longing threatened to swamp her. Dina closed her eyes tightly. Blake was fully aware of what he was doing to her. He had a motive for everything he did. She didn't believe that he was denying himself the possession of her out of respect, any more than she believed he had assigned Chet to help on the new project purely because she needed competent help. He wanted to undermine her trust in Chet. She vowed he wouldn't succeed.

But the aspersions Blake had made against Chet's character haunted her over the next two weeks. Again and again she cursed in silent protest at the seeds of doubt Blake had planted in her mind. The cold war between herself and Blake neither accelerated in those two weeks, nor was there even a hint of a thaw.

A knock at the opened door brought her out of her gloomy reverie. She had been staring out the dusty pane of the solitary window in her small office. She turned, slipping her reading glasses to a perch on top of her head.

"Hello, Chet." She stiffened at the sight of him and tried to relax, but she had become too self-conscious lately in his company, not feeling the same freedom and trust she had once found with him.

"I've finally got all the interior and exterior photographs of the hotels that you wanted." He indicated the stack of folders he was carrying with both hands. "I thought we should go over them together. Are you too busy to do it now?"

"No, bring them in." Dina began moving the papers from her desk. "Just give me a second to make some room."

Before the actual advertising campaign could begin, there was a lot of groundwork to be done. The most time-consuming part was improving the physical appearance of the hotels.

"I've already looked through them," Chet told her.

"Good," Dina nodded, and began to scan them herself.

The line of her mouth kept growing grimmer and grimmer. By the time she reached the bottom of the stack of photographs, she realized she had underestimated the amount of time and money it would take to superficially redo the hotels.

"It's worse than I thought," she sighed.

"Yes, I know," Chet agreed, matching her expression.

"Let's take the hotels one by one and make notes." She sighed. "The one thing we want to keep in mind is that each hotel should be different, its decor indigenous to its location. We don't want a vacationer to think that if he's been in one Chandler Hotel, he's been in them all."

"That's right."

"Okay, let's start out with the one in Florida." Dina gazed at the photographs. "I think it has to be the most challenging. I didn't realize it looked so sterile."

She flipped her glasses into place on her nose and reached for her note pad. 'Here we'll take advantage of the tropical environment. Heavy on wicker furniture, light and airy colors, no carpeting, cool tile floors, and lots of potted plants and greenery. Something like the decor in our Hawaiian hotel would be good, but without the Polynesian accent."

"What about the exterior?"

Dina thought of the budget and winced. "I hope we can get by with some landscaping. I don't want to do a major face lift unless there's no other way."

Down the list of hotels and their photographs

they went. The one in Maine would be done with a
nautical flavor. The one in Mexico would have a
lazy siesta look, complete with mock overhead fans
turning leisurely from the ceiling. The founding
hotel in Newport already had an elegant yachting
atmosphere, which would now be stressed. The
themes varied with each hotel, depending on its
location.

When the last photograph had been examined
and set aside, Dina looked at her copious collection
of notes and sighed at the dollar signs they meant.
She remembered her spiteful comment to Blake
about the interior decorating to be done, remarking
that it was woman's work. Well, there was a mountain of it here, one that she doubted Blake would
have the patience to tackle.

"Now what?" Chet questioned.

"Now—" Dina took a deep breath "—now we
need to have these notes transferred into sketches."

"Do you want me to start contacting some decorating firms?"

"I suppose so. With the scope of the work that
needs to be done, I'm just wondering how we
should handle it." She nibbled thoughtfully at her
lower lip. "Something, either major or minor, has to
be done at each of the hotels."

"In the past we've always used firms within the
area of the hotels, in the same city when we could,"
Chet reminded her.

"Yes, I know." Dina slid the pencil through the
platinum gold hair above her ear. "I checked the
records last week to get an idea of the possible costs
and noticed that in the past we'd always used local

firms. Before, it had proved to be both economical and good business to trade with a company in the same area as one of our hotels."

"But, since virtually all the hotels are involved, it might not be practical because of all the traveling that would have to be done," he observed. "That cost could eat into whatever savings we might realize by using a local decorator."

"I'm afraid you're right," she agreed with a rueful nod. "We might be better off with a major firm capable of doing all the work. In the long run it might prove to be the more economical choice."

"I tell you what—" Chet leaned forward, his blue gray eyes bright with suggestion "—first let's get these notes typed up. Then why don't I contact two major companies to give us estimates on the work? To get a comparison, I can pick a half dozen hotels that are fairly close to here and obtain bids from local firms. I can use the hotel in Maine, the one here in Newport, naturally, the one in the Poconos—I can check the list."

"That might work," she agreed, turning the idea over in her mind and liking it. It had been a half-formed thought in her own mind, but when Chet had spoken it aloud, it had solidified. "Excellent suggestion, Chet."

"I'll get started on it right away." He began gathering up the notes and the photographs from her desk. "We don't want to waste time."

"Before you go, there's something else I've been thinking about that I wanted to talk over with you to get your opinion," Dina said to detain him.

"What's that?" Chet sat back down.

"To keep this continuity of every hotel being individual, I think we should carry it into the restaurants," she explained.

"But we're doing that." He frowned. "There are going to be decor changes in the restaurants and lounges, too. We just went over them."

"No, I was thinking of extending the idea to the food."

"Do you mean changing the menus?"

"Not completely. We would have to keep the standard items like steaks, et cetera, but add some regional specialities, as well. We do it already along the coast with the seafood."

"I see what you're saying." Chet nodded. "In the Poconos, for instance, we could add some Pennsylvania Dutch foods. We could even carry it down to little touches, like serving genuine johnnycake made out of white cornmeal with the dinner rolls here in Newport."

"Exactly," Dina nodded.

"I'll contact the restaurant managers of all the hotels. Those that aren't already doing this can send us a list of three or four speciality dishes they can add to their menus," he suggested.

"Yes, do that. We can initiate this change right away by simply adding a flyer to the menus until new ones can be printed."

"Consider it done, Dina." He started to rise, then paused. "Is that all?"

"For now, anyway," she laughed.

"I'll be talking to you. And I'll have my secretary send you a copy of these notes," he promised, and gathered the stack of notes and photographs into his arms.

As Chet walked out of the office, the smile left Dina's face and was replaced by a wary frown. She stared at the open doorway, feeling those uneasy suspicions rearing their ugly heads. Then with a firm shake of her head she dismissed them and turned back to the papers she had been working on.

CHAPTER EIGHT

BENT OVER HER DESK, Dina was concentrating on the proposals from the selected advertising agencies. Absently she stroked the eraser tip of her pencil through her hair. Intent on the papers, she didn't hear the footsteps in the hallway or notice the tall figure darkening her open doorway.

"Are you planning to work late?"

The sound of Blake's voice jerked her head up. He stood there, so lithely powerful, so magnetically attractive. The darkness of his tan seemed to have faded little, its bronze hue accentuated by the white turtleneck sweater. Through half-closed lids he looked at her, creating the impression of lazy and friendly interest, yet his expression seemed masked.

As always when he caught her unaware, her pulse accelerated. An odd tightness gripped her throat, leaving her with a breathless sensation. For an instant the room seemed to spin crazily.

It was at moments like these that Dina wanted to let the powerful attraction she felt simply carry her away. But that was too easy and too dangerous. It wouldn't solve any of the differences that had grown in the years they were apart.

His question finally registered. She managed to tear her gaze away from his ever watchful eyes to glance at her wristwatch, surprised to see it was a few minutes before six o'clock.

Then she noticed the silence in the rest of the building. There were no muffled voices coming in from the hallway, no clackety-clack of typewriters. Nearly everyone had left for the day, except herself and Blake.

"I hadn't realized it was so late," she offered in answer to his question. "I just have to clear these things away and I'll be ready to leave."

As she stacked the proposals one on top of the other, preparatory to slipping them into their folder, Blake wandered into the room. He suddenly seemed to fill every square inch of it. Within herself, Dina was conscious of the sensuous disturbance his presence caused.

"How is the campaign progressing?" he inquired, his gaze flicking to the papers in her hand.

Dina had to search for the chilling antagonism that would keep him at a distance. "Hasn't Chet been keeping you informed?"

"No. Was he supposed to?" There was a baiting quality to the blandness of his voice.

"I presumed he would," she retorted, opening a desk drawer to put the folder away.

"If you didn't tell him to keep me up to date, Chet won't," said Blake, hooking a leg over the desk corner to sit on its edge. "He only does what he's told."

The desk drawer was slammed shut. "Will you stop that!" Dina glared at him.

"Stop what?" Blake returned with seeming ignorance.

"Stop making remarks like that about Chet!" The antagonism was there; she no longer had to search for it.

Blake made an indifferent shrug. "Whatever you say."

Impatiently she swept the remaining papers and pens into the middle drawer of her desk, leaving the top neat and orderly. Setting her bag on top, she pushed her chair up to the desk. Her sweater was lying on the back of the chair near where Blake stood.

"Hand me my sweater, please." Frigid politeness crept into her voice.

Glancing around, Blake slipped it off the chair back and held it out to her as she walked around the desk to the front. "How are you and Chet getting along?"

"The same as always—very well." Dina gave him a cool look and started to reach for the sweater. "Did you expect it to be different?" It was spoken as a challenge, faintly haughty. A light flashed in her mind and she forgot about the sweater. "You did expect it to change, didn't you?" she accused.

"I don't know what you're talking about."

"That's why you told Chet to give me a hand. I thought it was because you didn't think I could handle the job, but that wasn't it at all, was it?" Her anger was growing with each dawning thought.

Completely in control, Blake refused to react. "You tell me."

"You planted all those doubts in my mind about Chet, then made me work with him, hoping I would become poisoned against him. That's what this was all about, wasn't it?" Dina was incensed at the way Blake had attempted to manipulate her thinking.

"I admit that after our little talk about Chet, I

hoped the blinkers would come off and you would see him as he really is." There wasn't a trace of regret in his expression or his voice that his motive had been uncovered.

"That is the lowest, dirtiest thing I've ever heard!" she hissed.

Trembling with rage, she was completely unaware of her hand lashing out to strike him until it was caught in a vise grip short of its target. She gasped in pain as he twisted her arm to force her closer. He had straightened from the desk to stand before her, the sweater cast aside on the desk top.

"The last time you slapped me, I let you get away with it because I might have deserved it. But not this time," Blake told her flatly. "Not when I'm telling the truth."

"But it isn't the truth!" Dina flared, undaunted by his implied threat. "Not one word you've said against Chet is true. It's all lies. None of it is true!"

That darkly piercing look was back in his eyes as they scanned her upturned face. "You know it's true, don't you?" he breathed in a low, satisfied voice. "You've started to see it for yourself—that's why you're so angry."

"No, it isn't true," she denied. "I haven't seen it."

"You have. Why don't you admit it?" Blake insisted with grim patience.

"No," Dina continued to resist and strained to break free of his hold. "And I'm not going to stay here and listen to you tear Chet down anymore."

He increased the pressure of his grip and issued a taut denial. "I am not trying to make him appear less of a man. I'm trying to make you see him the way he is and not the way you've imagined him to be. Why can't you understand that what I'm saying is not a personal attack on him?"

Suddenly, unexpectedly, she did understand and she believed him. The discovery took the heat out of her anger. Dina stopped fighting him and stood quietly.

"All right," she admitted.

"All right what?" Blake lowered his gaze to her mouth, watching her lips as they formed the answering words.

"I have noticed a few things," Dina admitted further.

"Such as?"

"The way he takes a suggestion and elaborates on it until you're almost convinced the idea was his in the first place."

"He's done that?"

"Yes. Today, when I mentioned an idea I had about adding regional dishes to the restaurant menus." She wished Blake would stop watching her talk. It was unsettling, heightening her senses. "He's already contacting the restaurant managers to see about starting it."

"Chet is very good at organizing and carrying out a suggestion," Blake agreed. "What else?"

"I don't know. A lot of little things." The compliment Blake had given Chet prompted Dina to mention another conversation that had bothered her. "When I didn't take a stand today about having a local or a major decorating firm redo the hotels, Chet didn't either. He suggested getting comparison bids from both and avoided offering a concrete opinion. In the last two weeks, I honestly can't remember Chet making a decision or offering a proposal of his own."

Looking back, she realized that his proposal of marriage had been an outgrowth of a conversation about whether she would marry again or not. When she had coneded the possibility, Chet had asked if it would be someone like Blake she would choose. Her negative answer had then led to Chet's suggesting himself, after first testing out his ground.

That was hardly the mark of the strong, dependable man she had believed him to be. His reliability was limited to the times when someone else told him what to do.

Lost in her thoughts, Dina was unaware of the silence that had fallen between them until Blake spoke. "I have another equally selfish reason for wanting Chet to work with you on this project." His fingers were lightly stroking the inside of her wrist, a caressing motion that was disturbing.

A tingling warmth spread up her arm, her nerves fluttering in awareness of how close she stood to him. "What is it?" There was a breathless catch to her voice. She looked into his eyes, nearly overcome by the sensation that she could willingly drown in the dark pools.

"Because I know that eventually this project is going to entail a good deal of traveling and I wanted to make certain it wasn't my wife who went on these trips."

"I see." She couldn't think of anything else to say.

"You might as well know this, Dina," he said.

"You and I are never going to be separated for any reason."

The ruthlessly determined note underlying his statement made her shiver. There was a sense of being trapped, a feeling that his wishes were inescapable. Whatever Blake wanted, he got. But not from her, her pride protested—not unless it was her own decision to agree.

With a degree of reluctance, she withdrew from his touch, turning to the desk to pick up her sweater and handbag. "I'm ready to leave now," she said, aware of the conflicting magnetic currents between them, alternately pulling and repelling.

Blake didn't make a move to leave. He just stood there looking at her, making her feel more uncomfortable and unsure of her own wants and needs.

"Sooner or later you're going to have to make a decision," he told her.

"I know. Sooner or later," she echoed softly.

"Why are you waiting? What is holding you back?" he questioned. "It isn't Chet anymore, so what's left?"

"I don't know." Dina shook her head uncertainly.

Needing to move, she started for the door. With that animal silence she was beginning to associate with him, Blake came up behind her, his hands sliding over her shoulders. The mere touch of him stopped her in her tracks.

"Decide now," Blaked ordered in a low murmur.

The silvery gold length of her hair was secured in a bun low on the back of her head. She felt the warm stirring of his breath on the exposed skin of her neck, sensitive and vulnerable. The sensuous pressure of his lips exploring that special pleasure point sent a delicious tremor through her.

His hands slid down to her forearms, crossing them in front of her as he molded her shoulders, waist and hips to the hard contours of his body. Dina felt as pliable as putty, willing to be shaped into anything he wanted. Primitive passions scorched through her veins.

She struggled out of the emotional upheaval going on within her to protest, "Blake, I can't!"

"You want to." His mouth moved to her ear, his teeth nibbling at its lobe. "You know you do."

"I don't know anything," she breathed raggedly.

"Then feel," Blake instructed.

That was the problem. She felt too much and it blocked out her thinking processes. She didn't want to make a decision in the heat of an embrace. And certainly not in this inferno that was consuming her now.

"Blake, no!" She swallowed and pushed his hands from around her waist.

She took a step away from his tempting embrace and stopped, shaking and weak with desire. Her head was lowered, her chin tucked into her throat. She felt his gaze boring into her shoulders.

"Blake, no!" He mimicked her words with a biting inflection. "That's always your answer. How much longer are you going to keep giving it?"

"Until I'm absolutely sure that I know what I'm doing," Dina answered.

"And how long will that be?" Blake was striving for control. It was evident in the clipped patience of his tone.

"I don't know," she sighed. "I just know it's easy to surrender to passion now and not so easy to face tomorrow."

"Then you're a hell of a lot stronger than I am, Dina," he snapped, "because I don't give a damn about tomorrow!" He slipped a hand under her elbow. Her first thought was that he intended to ignore her uncertainties and kiss her into submission, something that would not be too difficult to do. Instead his hand pushed her forward. "Let's go," he muttered.

His long, ground-eating strides made it impossible for Dina to keep up with him without half running. The rigid set of his jaw kept her from drawing attention to herself or her plight. He didn't slow down until he reached the parking lot, where she struggled to catch her breath as they walked to the car.

Without looking directly at her, Blake unlocked the passenger door and held it open for her, slamming it shut when she was safely inside. Walking around the car, he unlocked his own door and slid behind the wheel. He put the key in the ignition, but didn't start the car.

Resting his hands on the steering wheel, he stared straight ahead for several long seconds, a forbiddingly hard line to his mouth. Dina grew increasingly uneasy at the silence and felt pinned when his dark glaze finally swung to her. It wasn't a pleasant sensation.

"The first day I was back," Blake said, "you claimed we needed time to get to know each other again—that we had to become adjusted to each other again. You felt we should talk."

"I'm surprised you remember," she remarked, and could have bitten off her tongue for issuing such caustic words.

"Believe me, I remember everything you've said," he returned with dry weariness, his attention shifting to the windshield in front of him. Dina shifted uncomfortably in her seat, but remained silent. "The point is, Dina, that we aren't getting to know each other again. We aren't talking. The only place we spend any time together alone is in the bedroom. And we both know there isn't any communication taking place there, physical or otherwise."

"So what are you suggesting? That we should communicate on a physical level and work on from there?" Dina questioned stiffly, her pulse quickening in a reaction that did not reject the idea.

"No, that isn't what I'm suggesting—" there was a cynical twist to his mouth "—although I know you're convinced that my instincts have become purely primitive."

A slight flush warmed her cheeks. "Then what are you suggesting?"

"That we spend more time together, as you wanted."

"That's a bit difficult with both of us working."

"Neither of us works on the weekend," Blake reminded her.

"You're forgetting we live in your mother's house." And Mother Chandler had still not got over her son's miraculous return. She still hovered around him every possible moment she could.

"No, I'm not," Blake returned calmly. "The key word is alone—no friends, no relatives, just you and

I. I realize that can't be accomplished in my mother's home. That's why I've decided we'll spend the weekend at Block Island so we can have the time alone together that you claim we need."

"Block Island." Dina repeated the name of the resort island located roughly fourteen miles off the Rhode Island coast.

"That's what I said. Any objections?" He turned his head to look at her, a challenging glitter in his dark eyes.

"None." How could there be when he had cornered her with her own words?

"There is one thing more, Dina." Blake continued to study her, aware of her reluctant agreement—although why it was reluctant, Dina didn't know.

"What's that?" She was almost afraid to ask.

"I want this clearly understood before we go. If you haven't made up your mind about us by Sunday night, I'm not waiting any longer." At the sight of her paling complexion, he smiled without humor. "And I don't care whether you consider that a threat or a promise."

"You can't make a deadline like that," she protested.

"Can't I?" Blake had already turned away to start the car, ignoring her now that he had stated his intentions.

"All you're doing is turning this weekend into a farce," Dina retorted.

"Call it what you like," Blake said indifferently. "Just be sure to pack a suitcase and bring it to the office with you Friday morning. We'll catch the ferry to Block Island after work."

As THE FERRY LEFT the protected waters of Narra-
gansett Bay for the open waters of the Atlantic
heading for the porkchop-shaped island offshore,
Dina stared sightlessly at the Brenton Reef Light
Tower. She and Blake had barely exchanged five
words with each other since leaving the office, and
the silence was growing thicker.

She knew the reason her lips were so tightly
closed. Blake's Sunday night ultimatum had made
her feel as if he was pointing a gun at her head. So
how could she look forward to the weekend ahead
of them? He had already foreordained the outcome,
so what was the purpose? She should have refused
to come. Why hadn't she?

Pressing a hand to her forehead, she tried to rub
away the dull throb. The pills she had taken to stave
off the sea sickness were working, but they clouded
her thinking processes. At least she had been spared
the embarrassment of being sick all over the place,
even if she did feel slightly drugged.

Sighing, she glanced at Blake standing a few
yards away talking to a fellow passenger. Their
attention was on the low-hanging, dull gray clouds
overhead. There was nothing menacing about them,
but they added to the gloom Dina felt.

The two were obviously discussing the weather,
because Dina overheard the man remark, "I hope
you're right that it's going to be sunny and clear at
the island. I don't know anything about ocean currents and how they affect the weather. All I know is
that I want to get a weekend of fishing in."

Blake's prediction of good weather on Block
Island proved correct. They were within sight of

their destination when the clouds began to thin, permitting glimpses of blue sky and a sinking yellow sun. When the ferry docked at the Old Harbor landing, there were only patches of clouds in the sky.

But the silence between Dina and Blake didn't break. Despite that, she felt her spirits lift as they drove off the ferry onto the island, named after Adrian Block, the first European to explore it. The island's atmosphere was refreshing and Dina understood why it had been a fashionable health spa in the Gay Nineties.

She became absorbed in the scenery as Blake drove across the island to the picturesque resort village of New Harbor stretched along the banks of the Great Salt Pond. It had once been an inland lake, but a man-made channel now linked it to the ocean, providing a spacious harbor for both pleasure craft and commercial fishing boats.

Much of the previous tension returned when Blake parked in front of a hotel. It seemed different somehow to share a hotel room. Just why, Dina couldn't say, since they'd been sharing a bedroom almost ever since Blake had returned. She felt self-conscious walking beside him into the lobby.

Blake glanced down at her, his gaze inspecting the discomfited look on her face. "How are you feeling?"

"Fine," Dina rushed out the answer.

"No leftover nausea from the ferry trip?"

"None. Actually I never felt I was going to be sick. Except for a slight headache, I'm fine," she insisted. "Either the pills are getting stronger or I'm finally outgrowing my sea sickness."

"Good." His smile was somewhat grim. "Excuse me. I'll go check on our reservation."

As he walked to the desk to register, she lingered near a rack of postcards, pretending an interest in their colorful pictures. There was a curling sensation in her stomach when she saw the porter take their bags. Blake walked toward her and she immediately picked a card from the rack, ostensibly to study it more closely.

"Were you planning to send a postcard to someone?" The cynically amused query didn't help her fluttering stomach.

"No." She quickly returned it to the rack. "I was just looking at the picture."

"Tomorrow we'll take a look at the real thing."

Dina had to glance at the postcard. She had been so conscious of Blake she hadn't noticed what the subject of the card had been. Now she saw it was a lighthouse.

"It looks interesting," she offered, just to be saying something.

"Yes," Blake agreed dryly, as if aware that she hadn't previously known what it was. "Shall we go to our rooms?"

"Rooms?" In the plural, her eyes asked.

"Yes, two," he answered. Dina was surprised by the gentle, almost tender expression of patience that crossed his usually hard features. "We have adjoining bedrooms. I intend to give this weekend every chance of proving whatever it is that you feel needs proving, Dina."

There didn't seem to be any response she could make. Strangely, this seemed more of a concession

than all the nights when Blake had shared her bed
without forcing an intimacy—perhaps because he
was granting her the privacy to think without his
presence to disturb or influence her.

When he handed her one of the keys in his hand,
she managed a quiet, "Thank you."

"When a man is desperate, he'll try anything,"
Blake returned cryptically, but Dina thought she
caught a glimmer of humor in his dark eyes. It
made him seem more human.

They walked to their rooms in silence, but it was
no longer as strained as it had been. Blake hesitated
outside his door, catching her eye for an instant
before he turned the key in his lock and walked in.

Entering her room, Dina noticed her suitcase
lying on the luggage rack and walked over to it,
intending to unpack. Instead, she paused at the
interior door that connected the two bedrooms.
Blake was on the other side of it. Unconsciously she
reached for the doorknob. It refused to turn; the
door was locked. Regret conflicted with relief as she
walked back to her suitcase and unpacked.

An hour later she had showered and was dressed
in a wheat-colored shirtwaist dress that was elegantly casual. Blake hadn't said whether he would
meet her at the restaurant for dinner or go down
with her. She debated whether she should wait in
the room or go to the restaurant, then decided to
wait and she sat down on the bed.

Instantly a smile curved her lips. The mattress
was blissfully soft, sinking beneath her weight like
feather down. It was going to be a wonderful
change from Blake's rock-firm mattress at the
house.

Just then there was a knock at her door and Dina rose to answer it, the smile lingering on her lips. Blake stood outside, his eyes warming to a dark brown at her expression.

"You look pleased at something," he commented.

"My bed," Dina explained, a pair of dimples etching grooves in her cheeks. "It's soft."

His chuckle of understanding was soft, almost silent—a disarming sight and sound. Her heart skipped a beat, then refused to return to an even tempo.

"Shall we go to dinner?"

It was more of a statement than a question as Blake held out his hand for hers. Self-consciously she let her fingers be engulfed in his hand, but he continued to block the doorway, not permitting her to step out. His hold on her hand shifted, raising the inside of her wrist to his mouth.

"Have I told you how very beautiful you are?" he murmured.

"Blake, please," Dina protested, her lashes fluttering down at the heady touch of his warm lips against the sensitive area of her wrist.

"It's simply a compliment," he interrupted with a wry smile as he brought her hand away. "All you have to do is say 'thank you.'"

"Thank you," she repeated in a tight little voice, more disturbed than she cared to acknowledge by the effect he had on her.

"That's better." Blake moved to the side, leading her out of the room and reaching behind her to close the hotel-room door.

Fresh seafood was the natural selection to make

from the menu. Once that decision had been made, Dina sat in the chair opposite from Blake. Inside she was a bundle of twisted nerves, but she forced herself to be still.

Without the steady chatter of Mother Chandler to lead a table conversation, she couldn't think of anything to say. It seemed an indication of how far she and Blake had grown apart. Her tongue was tied into knots.

"I'm going to have to make a trip to the bookstore soon," Blake commented with seeming idleness. "I have a lot of reading to catch up on."

"Yes, I suppose you do." Dina wanted to cry at how stilted her response had been.

But Blake either didn't notice it or deliberately ignored it. "It sounds a little crazy, I know, but reading was one of the things I really missed. More than good meals and clean clothes. I never considered it a necessity before."

"I doubt if I have, either," she admitted, forgetting her self-consciousness at his provocative comment.

"Any new titles you'd like to recommend?"

Dina hesitated, then suggested, *Roots*.

Before she realized what was happening, she found herself becoming engrossed in a discussion of new books that had been published in Blake's absence, and titles they had both read in the past. From reading, their conversation drifted to movies and Broadway shows. It seemed a natural progression to tell him about things she had done while he was gone, decisions she had been forced to make, such as subletting their apartment and sorting their furnishings.

When Blake later signaled their waiter for the check, Dina was astounded to discover that it was after ten o'clock and there had not been one awkward moment between them, not a single remark that had been in any way argumentative. She hadn't thought it was possible. She wondered if Blake had noticed it, but was afraid to ask. She didn't want to risk breaking whatever kind of temporary truce they had established.

They both seemed to be in a reflective mood as they retraced their way to their rooms. Dina was conscious of his hand lightly resting on the back of her waist, a faintly possessive air to his guiding touch, but she didn't object to it in the least.

"Do you know what this reminds me of?" Blake questioned her when they paused in front of her door.

"What?" Dina looked up, curious and thoughtful.

"All those times I used to walk you to the door of your sorority house and kiss you good night in a dark corner of the building." He glanced around the hallway, "Of course, here there aren't any dark corners." His gaze returned to her face. "But I *am* going to kiss you good night."

His head bent and Dina lifted hers to meet him halfway. The kiss was searingly light and questing, both seeking answers to unknown questions. Each seemed to realize that it would take only the slightest provocation to deepen the embrace to one of passion. Yet neither made it, merely testing the temperature of the water without becoming submerged in it.

With obvious reluctance they both withdrew from the embrace, gazing silently at each other. Blake took a step back, a closed look stealing over his face.

"Do you have your key?" he asked.

"Yes." Dina unfastened her clutch purse and took it out.

He hesitated a fraction of a second. "Good night, Dina." He moved toward his own door.

"Good night, Blake," she murmured, and entered her hotel room alone.

CHAPTER NINE

DINA DIDN'T SLEEP WELL that night. The irony of it was that it was because the mattress was too soft. She was wakened from her fitful dozing by a knock on the door and stumbled groggily across the room to answer it.

"Who is it?" She leaned tiredly against the door, her hand resting on the locked night latch.

"Blake," was the answer. "Are you ready for breakfast?"

Dina groaned. It couldn't possibly be morning already.

"Are you all right?" His tone was low and piercing.

"Fine," she mumbled, adding silently, *I just need some sleep.*

The doorknob rattled as he attempted to open it. "Unlock the door, Dina," he ordered.

She was too tired to think of a reason to refuse and too tired to argue if she had one. Slipping off the night chain, she unlocked the latch and stepped aside as Blake pushed the door open. Concern was written all over his expression, but she didn't notice.

"I don't want breakfast," Dina was already turning to make her way back to the bed. "You go ahead without me."

Blake's arm went around her to turn her back.

He pushed the tangle of corn-silk hair behind her ear and held it there, his hand cupping the side of her head and tipping it up. His strength was a glorious thing and Dina willingly let him support her weight, too weary to stand on her own.

"What's the matter, Dina? You look exhausted." Blake was frowning.

"I am," she sighed. "My beautifully soft bed was too soft. I barely slept all night."

He laughed softly. "Why didn't you take a pillow and blanket off the bed and sleep on the floor? Or was that too uncivilized for you?" He mocked her in a gently teasing voice.

"I suppose that's what you did?" Dina lifted her tired lashes to glance at him. He looked disgustingly refreshed and rested.

"Yes," he nodded.

"And probably slept like a baby," she added enviously.

"I didn't sleep all that well," Blake denied.

"Why not?" Dina slid her arms around his hard, warm body and rested her head against his shoulder, closing her eyes.

"I haven't liked sleeping alone since I met you."

His provocative statement sailed over her sleepy head. Dina was only aware of how very right it felt to be in his arms, so comfortable and so warm. She snuggled closer.

"Why don't you just hold me for a while and let me sleep?" she suggested in a sleepy murmur.

"I don't think so." The arm that had been around her withdrew to press a hand against her rib cage just below her breast to push her away. "If I hold you much longer, I won't be thinking about sleep," Blake stated, a half smile curving one corner of his mouth. "Why don't you shower and dress? I'll go get some coffee to help you wake up before we go to breakfast."

Dina didn't have a chance to agree or disagree. One minute she was in his arms and the next he was walking to the door, leaving her swaying there unsteadily. The closing of the door goaded her into movement. She looked longingly at the bed, but knew it was no use. Even if she could go back to sleep, Blake would be back shortly to waken her. Following his suggestion, she walked to the bathroom.

It was shortly after midmorning by the time Blake and Dina finished their breakfast and started out on a leisurely tour of the island, dotted with freshwater ponds. It was not the first visit for either of them, but it had been several years since their last.

There was little noticeable change on the island, with the possible exception that a few more trees had been planted by property owners. The young saplings looked forlorn in a landscape that was remarkably devoid of trees. Early settlers had long ago cut down the native ones for lumber to build their homes. Reforestation was a new and slow process.

Stone fences crisscrossed the rolling terrain. The rocks had been deposited on the island by glaciers from the Ice Age and stacked, probably long ago by slave labor, to erect property boundaries of early farms. They were a picturesque touch on the island, called by an early Italian navigator God's Little Isle.

On the southeastern shore Blake parked the car on Mohegan Bluffs. The picture-postcard lighthouse sat on the point of the bluffs, the rustic house and tower looking out to sea. Its navigational beacon was one of the most powerful on the New England coastline.

The salty breeze off the ocean was cool. Dina zipped the coral windbreaker up to her neck while Blake locked the car. Screeching seagulls soared overhead as they walked together past the lighthouse to the steep path leading down the headland to the beach.

A fisherman stood knee-deep in the surf, casting a fly line into the whitecaps. He nodded a friendly acknowledgment to them as they strolled by. Blake's arm was around Dina's shoulders, keeping her close to his side. She stepped over a piece of driftwood and turned her gaze up to his face. His features were relaxed with a look of contentment about them.

"Why are we getting along so well?" she mused, more to herself than to him.

"Maybe it's because we've stopped looking at each other," Blake suggested.

"What?" A bewildered frown creased her forehead, confusion darkening the blue of her eyes.

"It does sound a bit strange, doesn't it?" A faint smile touched his mouth when he glanced at her, then he directed his gaze ahead of them, a contemplative look about his expression. "What I think I mean is that we've stopped trying to see the flaws in each other, the differences. We've started looking outward together."

"Do you suppose that's it?" Dina, too, shifted her gaze to the beach in front of them.

"Why bother to analyze the reason?" he countered. "Why not just enjoy it?"

"That's true." She scuffed a canvas toe against a stone. "Except that I like to know the why of things."

"So I remember," Blake murmured dryly. "Like the time I gave you your engagement ring and you wanted to know what made me decide to propose to you."

Dina laughed. "And you said it was because I would make such a beautiful ornament in your home." The laughter died as she gave him a guarded look. "Is that the way you regard women? As ornaments?"

There was a hint of exasperation in his impatient glance. "You should know me better than that, Dina."

She was silent for several paces. "That's the problem, I guess—I'm not certain anymore how well I know you. You always seemed so cultured. Now—" she lifted her hand in a searching gesture "—you are so... earthy."

"I suppose I learned that the basics of life are more important. The rest is just window dressing. Fundamentally I don't believe I've changed."

"Perhaps I was so busy looking for the window dressing that I didn't recognize you," she wondered aloud.

"Perhaps," Blake conceded. He flashed her a

quick smile. "How did we get started on such a serious discussion?"

His lightning switch from a pensive mood to one that was lightly teasing was infectious. Dina responded immediately, "I don't know. You started it."

"No, I didn't. You did," he corrected her in the same light vein, "when you questioned why we weren't arguing."

"You didn't have to answer me, so therefore it's all your fault," she shrugged.

"Logic like that could only come from a woman," Blake declared with an amused shake of his head.

"Are you making disparaging remarks against my sex again?" she demanded in mock anger.

"I'm just stating facts," he insisted.

Dina gave him a sideways push with her shoulder. Knocked off balance, his arm slipped from around her and he had to take a step to one side to recover. Their aimless pace had taken them closer to the water's edge than either had realized, and when Blake took that step, his foot—shoe, sock and trouser cuff landed in salt water—Dina gasped in a laugh at the one wet foot.

"So you think its funny, do you?" He took a playfully threatening step toward her.

Unconsciously she began to retreat. "Honestly, Blake, I'm sorry." She was trying hard not to laugh, but it bubbled in her voice. "I didn't know. I didn't mean to push you in the water, honestly."

Blake continued to approach her. "Let's see if it's so funny when you get wet."

"Blake, no!" Dina kept backing up, swallowing

the laughter as she negatively shook the silver gold mane of her hair.

The wicked glint in his eye warned her that words would not appease him. Turning, she ran, sprinting for the rock bluff at a safer distance from the lapping ocean waves. Blake chased her, his long strides eating up her short lead. Any moment he would overtake her, Dina knew, and she spared a laughing glance over her shoulder.

A piece of driftwood in her path tripped her and sent her sprawling headlong onto the beach. Her outstretched arms broke most of her fall. Unharmed, she rolled onto her back, out of breath but still trying not to laugh, as Blake dropped to his knees beside her.

"Are you all right?" he asked, half smiling and half concerned.

"Fine," she managed to gasp.

Sitting on his heels, Blake watched silently as she caught her breath. But as her breathing slowed, her heartbeat increased. An exciting tension was leaping between them, quivering over her nerve ends in lightning stimulation.

Blake moved forward as if to assist her to her feet, but as he moved closer, arms bracing him above her, her lips parted, glistening moistly. Dina lifted her hands to his chest as if to resist him, but instead they slid around his neck, pulling him down.

Fire ignited at the hard pressure of his mouth, hungry and demanding. It spread through her veins, her bones melting under the intense heat. The weight of his body crushed her to the rocky sand. It was an exquisite pain. No part of her was immune to the fire Blake was arousing so thoroughly.

Reeling under the torrid assault of his desire, she knew she had lost control. She made no attempt to regain it, willing to let his lips dominate hers for as long as he chose. With each breath, she drew in the intoxicating scent of him, warm and magic, a fuel for the fire that consumed her.

Never had Dina felt so alive. Every corner of her heart was filled with love, overflowing and spilling out like a volcano. Any differences were burned away by the fiery embrace that transcended physical limits.

"Hey, mister?" She heard a child's voice when previously she had only been able to hear the pagan rhythms of their matching heartbeats. "Hey, mister!" This time the voice was more insistent and Blake dragged his mouth from hers to roll onto his side. "Have you seen my puppy?"

A young boy of six stood beside them, knees dirty, a baseball cap on his light brown hair, staring at them innocently. Dina could feel Blake gathering the control to answer him.

"No, son, I haven't." His reply was tight and brief to conceal the raggedness of his breathing.

"He's white and black with a red collar," the boy explained.

"Sorry, we haven't seen him," Blake repeated patiently.

"If you do, would you bring him back to me?"

"Sure."

"Thanks." And he trotted off, disappearing around a jutting promontory on the beach.

Blake stared in the direction the boy had taken. "A few more seconds and it could have been embarrassing," he remarked grimly. "Come on." Rolling to his feet, he caught at Dina's hand to pull her along with him.

"Where are we going?" There was a faint pink to her cheeks.

"Back to the hotel."

"Why?"

"You're forgetting," he answered accusingly, flashing her a look that still had the smoldering light of desire. "I have a wet shoe, sock and pant leg."

Slightly subdued, Dina offered, "I'm sorry about that."

"I'm not." His finger touched her lips, tracing their outline, warm and still throbbing from his possession of them. "If that's what I get for a wet foot, I can't help wondering what would happen if I'd been drenched from head to toe." She breathed in sharply, wanting to tell him he didn't have to wait to find out, but she simply couldn't say the words. Blake didn't wait for her to speak, removing his fingers from her lips to encircle her hand. "Let's go, shall we?"

Dina nodded in silent agreement.

The magic moment lay between them on their return trip to the hotel, the irrevocable change it had made unspoken. But it was there in the looks they exchanged, in the things they didn't say and in the way they avoided physical contact with each other. They each seemed to know how combustible a touch could be and were not ready to start a false fire.

Neither of them was willing to acknowledge the change in the relationship. At the same time, they couldn't go back to the cold hostility that had preceded the visit to the island. They each played a waiting game.

After a late lunch in the hotel restaurant, they entered the lobby. Blake stopped short and turned to Dina. "We're checking out and going home," he announced.

"It's only Saturday," she protested.

"Yes. I know," he agreed with a hint of impatience. "But I'm not looking forward to spending another night here."

Dina hesitated, uncertain of his meaning. Finally she acknowledged. "The beds aren't very comfortable."

His mouth twisted wryly. "Yes, they're too soft."

"Do we have time to catch the ferry?"

"If you don't waste too much time packing, we do," he told her.

"I won't," she promised.

"I'll check out while you get started," said Blake.

During the ferry crossing neither mentioned the abrupt change of plans that had them returning early. They talked around it as if unwilling to delve too deeply into the reason. When the ferry docked in Newport they stopped talking altogether, both absorbed in their own thoughts.

It was several seconds before Dina noticed that Blake had missed a corner. "You were supposed to turn at that last block," she reminded him.

"We aren't going back to the house right away," he said.

Dina waited for him to tell her their destination. When he didn't, she asked, "Where are we going?"

"There's something I want to show you," was all he answered.

After several more blocks, he turned onto a tree-shaded street, branches arching overhead, nearly touching. He slowed the car down, seeming to read the house numbers as he drove down the street. Dina's curiosity grew with each second of his continued silence. Finally he turned into a driveway and stopped the car, switching off the engine.

Dina glanced at the large white house surrounded by a green lawn with lots of trees and flowering shrubs. She didn't recognize the place.

"Who lives here?" she asked.

Blake was already opening his car door and stepping outside. "You'll see."

She flashed him a look of irritation as he came around to open her door. He was carrying all this mystery business just a little too far. But she said nothing and walked ahead of him along the winding sidewalk to the front door.

There was a jingle of metal behind her and she turned. Blake was taking a set of keys from his pocket. Selecting one, he stepped ahead of her and inserted it in the front-door lock. Suspicion glittered in her eyes.

Pushing the door open, he motioned to her. "Go on in."

Her gaze swerved to the opened door as she moved forward to cross the threshold. On her right, carved oak posts ran from floor to ceiling to partition the mock entryway from the spacious living room beyond. Although the room was sparsely furnished, the items that were there Dina recognized as furniture stored from their apartment.

"What is this supposed to mean?" Unable to look at him, she thought she already knew the answer, and his high-handedness made her tremble with anger.

"Do you like it?" Blake ignored her question to ask one of his own.

"Am I to presume you bought this house without consulting me?" she demanded accusingly in a low, shaking voice, barely able to control her ire.

"As I recall, you were too busy to be bothered with looking for a place for us to live or furnishing it," he reminded her in an expressionless tone. "But to answer your question—no, I haven't signed any documents to purchase this house."

"If that's true, what is all our furniture doing here?" Her hand waved jerkily to the sofa and chairs.

"I obtained permission from the owner to have it brought in to see how it would fit in the rooms and to give the decorator an idea of what still has to be done."

Dina turned on him roundly, her eyes flashing fire. "In other words, you're presenting me with an accomplished fact! It doesn't matter what I want! You've decided on this house and if I don't like it, that's just too bad, isn't it?"

"Your opinion does matter." A muscle was twitching along his jaw, the only outward sign that he felt the lashing of her words. "That's why I brought you here."

There was a skeptical lift of her chin, disbelief glittering in her eyes despite his smooth denial. "Why not? Why not before? All this furniture wasn't just brought here and arranged overnight."

"No, it wasn't," Blake agreed.

"Then why now?" Dina repeated her demand.

"Because I had the impression you were ready to start looking for a place we might share together."

His narrowed gaze was piercing, impaling her on its point until she wanted to squirm under his sharp scrutiny. She averted her attention to the room, unable to admit that it might have been more than an impression.

"Was I wrong, Dina?" Blake questioned.

She didn't want to answer that question—not yet, not until she had more time to think about it. She didn't want to be manipulated into a commitment.

"Since I'm here, you might as well show me through the rest of the house," she said with forced indifference.

Blake hesitated, as if to pursue the answer to his question, then gestured with his hand. "The dining room and kitchen are this way," he directed.

As Dina toured the house, she realized it was everything they had ever talked about in a home of their own. Spacious without being too large, with ample room for entertaining, a study for Blake where he could work undisturbed in the evenings, a large patio in back, and plenty of closets.

"Since you're working, I thought we could arrange to have a maid to come in and do the housework," Blake explained as they walked down the hallway from the master bedroom to the main living area of the house.

"Yes," Dina agreed absently. At the open doorway of one of the two empty rooms, she paused to look inside again. The spare bedrooms were smaller than the master bedroom, but stil adequately large.

"There is one thing I haven't asked you." Blake stopped beside her.

"What's that?" She turned to meet his gaze.

"I haven't asked how you felt about having children."

Slightly flustered, Dina looked back to the empty room, visualizing it not as a guest bedroom but as a children's room. "We've talked about it before." They had discussed having two children, possibly three, she remembered.

"That was several years ago," Blake pointed out, "before you became a career woman."

"Working women raise children." She hedged, avoiding a direct answer and speaking in generalities instead.

"And there are some working women who prefer not to have children," he added. "I'm asking what you prefer, Dina."

He seemed to silently demand that she look at him. Reluctantly she let her gaze swing back to him, but she was unable to look any higher than his mouth. There were no soft curves to it; it was strong and firm and masculine. Dina had the impulse to raise her fingertips to it and trace the strength of its outline.

"I would like to have children, yes." Her reply was soft, almost inaudible.

"Do you have any objections to my being their father?" There was a husky quality to his voice.

The movement of his mouth when he spoke broke the spell and Dina looked away, her heart pulsing erratically. She didn't make a response. She couldn't seem to speak. Something was blocking her voice.

"Do you?" Blake repeated. When she remained silent, his fingers turned her chin to force her to look at him. "Was I mistaken this afternoon on the beach?" His steady gaze didn't waver as he looked deeply into her eyes, seemingly into her very soul. "Did you give me your answer, or was it a fleeting surrender to passion?"

"I don't know." Dina wanted to look away, but she couldn't. Her mind was reeling from his touch, incapable of coherent thought. "I ... I can't think."

"Just this once, don't think" Blake requested. "Tell me what you're feeling."

His hands slipped to her shoulders, tightening for a fraction of a second as if he wanted to shake the answer out of her, but they relaxed to simply hold her. Dina stared into the bluntly chiseled features, leather-tanned, and those compelling dark eyes. This was Blake, a man, her husband, and not quite the stranger she had thought him to be.

She swayed toward him and he gathered her into his arms, prepared to meet her more than halfway. Her lips parted under the plundering force of his mouth, taking the prize she so readily surrendered to him. As if it had never been away, her soft shape molded itself to the hard contours of his body.

His roaming hands caressed and shaped her ever closer to his solidly muscled flesh. Their combined body heat melted them together, fusing them with the glorious fire of their love. His driving male need made Dina aware of the empty aching in the pit of her stomach, which only he could satisfy.

Soon the torrid embrace was not enough. It was unable to meet the insatiable needs of their desires. Bending slightly, Blake curved an arm under her knees to lift her bodily and carry her to the master bedroom and the bare mattress of their old marriage bed.

As he laid her on the bed, the twining arms around his neck pulled him down to join her. Nothing existed for either of them but each other—not the past and not the future, only the moment, eternally suspended in time.

The inital storm of their passion was quickly spent. When Blake came to her a second time, their lovemaking was slow and languorous. Each touch, each kiss, each intimate caress was enjoyed and prolonged, savored and cherished.

The beauty of it brought tears to Dina's eyes, jewel-bright and awesomely happy. Blake kissed them away, gently, adoringly. Never had it been like this between them, as near to perfection as mere mortals can get.

Blake curved her to his side, locking his arms around her. Dina sighed in rapturous contentment and snuggled closer, not wanting to move, never wanting to move. Here was where she belonged, where she would always belong.

CHAPTER TEN

BLAKE STROKED HER HAIR, absently trailing his fingers through the silken ends, watching the fairness of its color glisten in the light. Her eyes were closed in supreme contentment.

"Would you say it now, Dina?" His huskily caressing voice rumbled from deep within his chest.

"Say what?" she questioned in equal softness, not sure words could express anything close to what she was feeling.

"Welcome home, darling." He supplied the words he wanted to hear.

Tipping back her head, she looked up to his face, love bringing a dazzling brilliance to the blue of her eyes. "Welcome home, darling." She repeated the words in a voice that trembled with the depth of her meaning.

A strangled moan of a torment ending came from his throat as he lifted her the few inches necessary to plant a hard, possessive kiss on her lips. Then his trembling fingers moved over her lips as if to apologize for hurting them.

"I've been waiting so long to hear that." There was a sad, almost wistful curve to his strong mouth. "Now, it doesn't seem nearly as important."

"A thousand times I've wondered if it might not have been different if I'd known you were alive before I saw you at the house," Dina whispered, her heart aching at the time together they had lost. "I thought it was someone's twisted idea of a joke."

"I should have made more of an effort to get hold of you or have the authorities reach you before I came back," Blake insisted. "I knew it would be a shock. Chet tried to convince me to let him break the news to you, but I didn't listen, not even when my own mother was so stunned that she didn't believe it was me. I was expecting too much not to think you would react the same way. In the end I went to my mother, but I tried to make you come to me."

"It wasn't just shock," she explained. "It was guilt, because I'd become engaged to Chet. And there you were, my husband. I wanted to run to you, but I couldn't. Then suddenly, you seemed so different—a stranger, someone I didn't know. It was window dressing," Dina sighed.

"Subconsciously I didn't want to admit there'd been any changes in either of us," he murmured with a rueful smile. "I wanted everything to be the way it was, as if I'd never been gone."

"Still, everything might have been different if I hadn't been engaged to Chet." Dina turned to rest her head again on his bronzed chest and listen to the strong rhythm of his heartbeat.

"It might have made us less wary of each other, but we still would have had to adjust to our growth as human beings. It would have been painful under any circumstances," he insisted.

"Yes, but Chet—" Dina started to argue.

Blake interrupted. "He was never a threat to our

relationship. Even if I hadn't come back, I'm convinced you would never have married him. You might have drifted along with the engagement for a year, but you're much too intelligent not to eventually have seen that it wouldn't work."

She relaxed, suddenly knowing he was right, and the last little doubt vanished. Smiling, she slid her hand over his flat, muscular stomach, as smooth and hard as polished bronze.

"Weren't you just a little bit jealous of Chet?" The question was half teasing and half serious.

"No, I was never jealous of him," he chuckled, and tugged at a lock of hair.

"Never?" Dina was almost disappointed.

"Never," Blake repeated in an absolutely positive tone. "There were times, though, when I was envious."

"Why?"

"Because you were so natural with him, so warm and friendly, trusting him, relying on him, and turning to him when you were confused. I wanted it to be me," he explained. "A man's instinct to protect is as strong as the maternal instinct in a woman. That's why I was envious of Chet—because you wouldn't look to me for security."

"I feel very secure now." Dina hugged him. "I love you, Blake. I've never stopped loving you."

"That's what I really wanted to hear." His arms tightened around her, crushing her ribs. "Welcome home was just a substitute for I love you."

"I love you," she repeated. "You don't have to prompt me into saying that. I shall keep saying it until you get sick of it."

"Never, my love." He shook his head.

There was a long silence as they reveled inwardly at the rediscovery of their love and the eloquently simple words that expressed so much.

"I hate to bring up something so mundane," Dina whispered, "but where are we going to sleep tonight?"

"I don't even want to go to sleep," said Blake.

"Aren't you tired?" Her sleepless night on the soft mattress was beginning to catch up with her, aided by the dreamy contentment of his embrace.

"Exhausted," he admitted with a smile in his voice. "But I'm afraid if I go to sleep, I'll wake up and find none of this has happened. Or worse, that I'm still in the jungle."

"If you are, I'm going to be there with you," she declared, and poked a finger in his chest. "You Tarzan, me Jane." Blake chuckled and kissed her hair. "Seriously, Blake, are we going back to the house tonight?"

"Not if the storage boxes in the garage have any blankets in them. Do they?" he questioned.

"Did you take everything out that I had in storage?"

"Every single solitary thing," he confirmed.

"Then there are blankets in the boxes in the garage," she promised. "As a matter of fact, there's everything there needed to set up housekeeping."

"Is that what you'd like to do?" Blake asked. "Stay here tonight?"

"I thought you'd already decided we were."

"I'm asking if that's what you want to do," he explained patiently.

"I must remember that and mark it on the calendar," Dina murmured. "Blake asked me what I wanted to do instead of telling me what I was going to do."

"All right, troublemaker," he laughed. "You know what I'm really asking."

"You want to know whether I like the house?" Dina guessed, propping herself up on a elbow beside him.

"Do you?"

"Yes. As a matter of fact, I love it," she smiled. "It's everything we ever said we wanted in a house."

"Good. That's what I thought, too. Monday morning I'll have the agent draw up the papers for us to sign. In the meantime, I don't think he'll mind if we start unpacking the boxes in the garage."

"What if he sells it to somebody else?"

"He won't. I put earnest money down to hold it until you saw it and, I hoped, approved of my choice."

"Were you so positive I'd like it?"

"As positive as I was that you'd love me again," Blake answered.

"Conceited!" Dina teased. "It would serve you right if I hadn't liked it."

"But you do, and now you can take over the decorating of it."

"It might end up looking like a hotel," she warned.

"It better not," he laughed, and pulled her into his arms.

THERE WAS A SCATTERING of snowflakes outside her office window, falling from pearl gray clouds. A serenely joyful light was in Dina's eyes as she smiled at the telephone receiver she held to her ear.

"Thank you, I'll tell him," she promised. "Merry Christmas."

Hanging up, she let her attention return to the papers on her desk while absently humming a Christmas carol. The interoffice line buzzed and she picked up the telephone again.

She had barely identified herself when Blake ordered crisply, "I want you in my office immediately."

"What's it about?"

"We'll discuss it when you get here."

An eyebrow arched at his sharpness. "Very well," Dina agreed calmly. "Give me about fifteen minutes."

"I said now," he snapped.

"You're forgetting it takes that long to walk from my little cubbyhole to your office," she reminded him dryly.

"Now, Dina!" And the connection was broken.

Breathing in deeply, she stared at the dead phone before finally replacing it on its cradle. She took a few precious seconds to put her desk into some kind of order, then walked into the corridor, closing her office door as she left.

Her statement of fifteen minutes was an exaggeration. Eight minutes later, Amy Wentworth glanced up from her typewriter and motioned her into Blake's office with a greeting wave of her hand. Dina knocked once on the connecting door and opened it to walk in.

Blake sat behind his desk leaning back in his

chair when Dina entered. The bluntly male features still retained much of his tropical tan, but they were drawn into coldly harsh lines to match the temperature outdoors. Anger glittered in his dark eyes and Dina had no idea why.

"You wanted to see me, Blake?" She walked to his desk, smiling warmly at her husband, but it didn't thaw his expression. "Am I being called on the carpet about something?"

"You're damned right you are!" He reached forward to shove a paper across his desk toward her, his glittering and watchful gaze never leaving her face for an instant. "What's this all about?"

Dina reached for the paper and glanced over it. "This is the revised budget request," she answered, frowning as she recognized it. "Where did you get it?"

"From Chet," Blake snapped.

Her mouth became a straight line of grim exasperation. "He wasn't supposed to give it to you. I wanted to go over it with you when I submitted it."

"He didn't give it to me, I took it. And you can go over it with me now," he ordered. "This is the—what—third or fourth budget revision?"

"The third." Dina was determined not to match his biting tone. "And if you'd told me why you wanted to speak to me, I could have brought some suppporting papers."

"I'm not interested in supporting papers, I want an explanantion. What's the cause for the increase this time? And don't tell me it's inflation."

"It's a combination of things," she began. "We had to change advertising agencies for the campaign because the original firm wasn't able to produce due to some internal problem. That meant an increase in the cost."

"You should have checked more thoroughly into the first company," he rebuked her.

"Their difficulties occurred after we'd signed a contract with them," she replied sharply to his criticism.

There was disbelief in his look, but he didn't pursue that aspect. "What else?"

"We had to revise the cost figures on revamping the hotels. The—"

"I knew it," he declared through clenched teeth. "The redecorating costs for the hotels have escalated every time you've submitted a budget. Are you redecorating them or rebuilding?"

The slow-burning fuse of her temper was lit. "There are times when I'm not so positive myself," she said, simmering. "Have you seen that hotel in Florida? It looks like a hospital. We've tried landscaping and painting, but it needs a whole new facade."

"Why don't you just arrange to tear it down and build a new one?" he flashed.

"That's the best suggestion I've heard yet!" she retorted. "Why don't you bring that up to the expansion department?"

"At the rate you're going, it might be the most economical decision!" With controlled violence, Blake pushed out of his chair, standing behind the desk to glance at her. "I should have known this would happen. You put a woman in charge and give her a free hand, and right away she thinks it means she has a blank check!"

Hot tears burned her eyes. "If that's what you think—" pain strangled her voice "—why don't you take over? I never asked for the job in the first place! If you think a man can do so much better, go ahead!"

"And don't think I couldn't!"

"The great Blake Chandler. Oh, I'm sure you could do a much better job," Dina issued sarcastically, and turned away, hugging her arms in front of her in a mixture of disgust and hurt. "I don't know what ever made me think I'd want your baby."

"I don't know, either!" Blake snarled behind her. "It's a lucky thing you have a choice, isn't it?"

"That's the whole point! I don't have a choice anymore," she cried bitterly.

Her sentence hung in the air for a long, heavy second before Blake broke the silence with a low demand. "What did you say?"

"Didn't I tell you?" She tossed the question over her shoulder, her chin quivering with the forced attempt at lightness. "I'm going to have a baby."

In the next second his hands were on her shoulders to gently turn her around. Dina kept her chin lowered, still angry and hurt by his barbed attack.

"Are you sure?" he asked quietly.

"Yes, I'm sure." She closed her eyes to try to force back the tears. "Doctor Cosgrove called me a few minutes ago to confirm the test results."

"Why didn't you tell me?" His tension was exhaled with the question.

"How could I when you've been yelling at me for the past five minutes?" Her eyes flared open to glare at him.

His fingers lightly touched her cheek before he cupped it in his hand. "I was, wasn't I?" There was a rueful twist to his mouth.

"Yes, you were." But her assertion didn't carry any sting of anger.

"I lost my perspective for a moment, the order of importance. I could lose everything I have and it wouldn't matter as long as I didn't lose you."

The glow radiating from his face was warm and powerful and Dina basked in the love light. That serene joy she had known before their argument returned with doubled strength.

"No, it doesn't matter as long as I have you," she agreed, and turned her lips to his hand to press a kiss into his open palm.

His head lowered, his mouth claiming hers in a sweetly fierce kiss that rocked her senses. She clung to him, reveling in the possessive embrace that gathered her close to his male length. A wild, glorious melody raced through her veins, its tune timeless, the universal song of love.

She was breathless when the kiss ended, and the sensation remained as Blake buried his face in the silver gold hair, his mouth trailing a blazing fire to the sensitive skin of her neck. She felt the tremors vibrating through his muscular form and knew she disturbed him as sensually as he disturbed her.

When he finally lifted his head, there was a disarming smile softening his roughly carved features. His hands moved to tangle his fingers in her hair and hold her face up for his gaze to explore. Dina knew this was a moment she would treasure forever in her heart.

"We're really going to have a baby?" There was a faintly marveling look in his eyes as Blake turned the statement into a near question.

"Yes," Dina nodded.

"Are you all right?" he frowned.

"I'm fine." She smiled. With a sighing shake of her head, she asked, "Why do we argue so much, Blake?"

"It's our nature, I guess." He smiled wryly in return. "We'd better get used to the fact, because we'll probably do it the rest of our lives."

"Always testing to find out which of us is stronger." Dina recalled Chet's explanation for their constant quarrels.

"Don't worry, honey, I'll let you be stronger once in a while," he promised.

"Blake!" She started to protest indignantly at his superior remark.

"Can you imagine what our children are going to be like?" he laughed. "Pigheaded, argumentative little rebels, more than likely."

"More than likely," Dina agreed, "And we'll love every battling moment of raising them."

"The same as every battling moment you and I have together." He kissed her lightly and gazed into her eyes. "When's the baby due?"

"July."

"The new campaign will be in full swing by then. I can just see you directing operations from the maternity ward," Blake chuckled.

"You mean that I still have the job?" Dina arched a mocking brow at him.

"Of course," he returned with an arrogant smile.

"Aren't you glad you have an understanding boss who will let you set your own hours or work at home, if that's convenient?"

"I'm very lucky." She slid her arms around his neck, rising on tiptoes. "Lucky in more than one way."

"Dina." Blake spoke her name in an aching murmur against her lips.